For Deborah Jockel,
who showed me myself

CONTENTS

1

AWKWARD BEGINNINGS

Yasmin drew her legs up onto the broad window seat and hugged her knees to her chest. The breeze block wall was rough and gritty against her back and her bare feet slid a little on the warm, polished wooden seat. Afternoon sunshine flooded the small college room, and the sky beyond the smooth lawns and stately lime trees was a clear, vivid blue. Closing her eyes, she concentrated on the heat of the sun beating through the long window and tried to forget the letter to her mother lying unfinished on the desk. She could hear the dull beat of music playing in another room and the occasional distant slam of a door on the floor below.

Suddenly voices burst onto the corridor, laughing, excited women's voices, talking in two or three different conversations, of which she caught only a few words:

"...Oh God, I was so embarrassed!..."

"...he wrote to her every week over the summer..."

"...three o'clock on Friday afternoons, it's to stop us sloping off early at the weekend. I hate him..."

Yasmin listened curiously as the voices drifted towards her room, but before they reached her, a key rattled in the lock of a room across the corridor. The voices were swallowed up in the quiet click of a door closing, leaving an echoing silence in the empty corridor.

She felt a stab of disappointment. How could she write to her mother and say that she had been here three days and still knew no-one in her hall? It was harder to meet people than she had imagined. She felt shy about just leaping out and introducing herself when she heard someone on the corridor, and they always sounded so busy with their own friends. She stared through smeared glass at the empty gravel paths and flat green lawns and thought about home. On a fine Sunday afternoon like this

Mum and Rod would be out walking, up on Moscar Moor, where fresh buffeting winds snatch your breath away and soft layers of blue hills fade to the horizon...

She remembered the last day before she left for university.

"Your last day before the Big Adventure!" Rod had teased her as they all walked briskly across open moors towards the crags she knew so well. She was so excited she could hardly contain herself.

"I know you'll be sensible, love, but do be careful when you go to parties, people might encourage you to try all sorts of things and they'll be looking for new students like you," her mother counselled, anxiously.

"Give over, Maggie," Rod scoffed. "Students these days are hard-headed capitalists, hell-bent on careers as stockbrokers and brain surgeons, there are no pot-smoking hippies left in the world."

"Thank you very much!" Yasmin interrupted, laughing indignantly. "But you don't know anything about it, I'm the one who's going and I'll tell you what students these days are like when I am one!" and she took a running jump at a large puddle of dank water and landed squarely on the soft peat at the far side. Maggie followed precipitately and landed with a loud splat a little short of the edge. She clutched wildly at Yasmin to pull herself clear, as they both dissolved into giggles. Rod skirted the edge carefully, teetering on precarious clumps of heather.

Later her friend, Jenny, came round to help with the final packing. They sat on the floor in Yasmin's attic room, sipping wine Maggie had bought for the occasion and listening to old tapes of chart songs from their early teens when they had first started going to discos.

"It's going to be so boring without you," Jenny moaned tragically. "What am I going to do with myself?"

"You've always got Annette!" Yasmin consoled mischievously, and they laughed wickedly at the thought of the person they both loathed most in the whole universe. They bickered about whether to put the shirts or the jeans on top, and where to put Yasmin's oily bicycle

8

repair kit. Right at the end, Jenny produced a small square present wrapped in flowery paper, which she insisted was not to be opened until Yasmin got there...

Yasmin could see it now, hanging on the wall above the chest of drawers, a small framed photograph of the Derbyshire moors in the snow, glistening white beneath a leaden sky, a quietly insistent reminder of home.

"Come on, get a grip, Yasmin," she whispered, her voice sounding strangely hoarse in the silence. She stood up decisively and padded across to the desk, where she picked a tape from a neatly stacked pile and put it in her small radio cassette player. Slowly and gently, the familiar, warming reggae beat seemed to wash away the silence and mingle with the sunlight around her, teasing her into a lighter mood. She settled herself before the letter again and began writing.

`It's Sunday now and I should have posted this yesterday, but I've been SO BUSY!! You'll be amazed to hear I'm very organised in my little room now - though I'm hardly ever here, of course. Freshers' Week was just manic and it's a relief to have a quiet Sunday to recover from all the discos and parties and stuff. I've met loads of really nice people on my course, and last night me and these other two girls went out - '. She paused guiltily for a moment, remembering how she had dressed up to go to the Freshers' Disco the night before. Sitting at her desk making pointless notes on her Students' Handbook, she had told herself it was too late and she would have missed the two girls from her linguistics course who said they would meet her in the bar. `But I have to tell her something,' she thought, and continued writing.

`- and we had a brilliant time. It's a lovely sunny day today, I'm going out on my bike in a bit to see what sort of area this is. It seems a bit boring and suburban, but there's a park nearby which looks quite nice, and lots of trees everywhere.

`Hope you're all surviving without me - does Tibby miss me? There's a cat just like her in the old lodge by the...'

A loud knock on the door interrupted Yasmin and startled her from her seat. She hurried to open the door, glancing quickly at the mirror above the washbasin to check her dark, shoulder-length hair was not too tangled. She took a deep breath and turned the handle. Outside two young women were waiting, one slight and dark-haired, the other taller with a large face framed by bushy light brown curls. Yasmin recognised them immediately as Trish and Sharon from her course.

"Hiya!" Trish smiled. "We wondered what happened when you didn't turn up last night. We've come to check you're all right."

"Oh, I'm fine," Yasmin laughed brightly. "Come in."

She showed them into the room and quickly whisked her dressing gown off the low square armchair so that Trish could sit down. Trish threw her denim jacket onto the back of the chair. Slumping comfortably into the sagging foam seat, she began to look around, her pale, thin face alive with curiosity. Sharon sat on the window seat, one leg tucked under her faded cotton dress, the other raised onto the seat, her arm resting across her knee. Yasmin felt overdressed and old-fashioned in her beige trousers and cream shirt and wished she had worn jeans. She couldn't imagine herself ever wearing an old dress and black leggings like Sharon, sitting there looking so laid back and matching so perfectly Yasmin's image of a typical student. She felt ridiculously excited and flustered having her lonely room suddenly invaded like this and was pleased she already had some music playing. She hoped the atmosphere was welcoming and relaxed.

As she hung her dressing gown on the back of the door, Yasmin asked them if they wanted a drink. They both wanted tea, so she filled her new electric kettle - with some difficulty as the taps in the washbasin were not angled to fit a kettle beneath them - and left it to boil on the cork-tiled floor by the desk. She turned the upright chair round and perched on the edge of it, facing her guests with the sun dazzling her eyes.

"So what happened about the disco, then?" Trish

persisted, running her fingers back through her sleek hair in a gesture that emphasised its fineness. "Find better company than us, did you? Don't tell me you've got a bloke already?" There was a teasing note in her voice and Yasmin found it hard to judge if she was amused or annoyed.

"Give us a chance, we've only just got here!" she laughed, slightly embarrassed. "Actually, I didn't feel very well after supper, the stew they gave us was disgusting. I'm really sorry, I hope you weren't waiting too long."

"Oh, that doesn't matter," Sharon said warmly. She had a slow, lazy way of talking, with a slight West Country accent. "The bar was better than the disco, anyway! How are you feeling this morning?"

"Much better," Yasmin replied, avoiding looking at either of them. She got up again, distractedly, and began searching in the bottom of her wardrobe for the teapot and mugs she and her mother had bought only a week before in a last-minute shopping spree. `Mum was right about having lots of mugs,' she thought, excitedly, `students do pop in and out of each others' rooms all the time.' She found the mugs and quickly peeled off the price stickers behind the wardrobe door so that Trish and Sharon wouldn't notice that they had not been used.

"It's a shame you're stuck over here," Sharon said. "It's great in our hall 'cos we're nearly all first years. But Fiona's right out in a house in Burton Lees with second years and she hates it, they've all got their own friends. How do you get on with them over here?"

"Everyone's fine," Yasmin lied. "I was lucky to get a place in hall at all, I applied so late, I knew I wouldn't get a place in Wentworth. I don't think everyone's back here yet and some of them are probably third years so they've got a lot of work on."

"I doubt it!" Trish laughed. "My brother's a third year at Aston and he's a right dosser, they just go out all the time and scive lectures. That's what he says anyway."

Yasmin rinsed out her own Snoopy mug and filled the

11

shiny purple teapot from the kettle. "I'll just get some milk," she muttered and hurried off down the corridor to the kitchen. The light was on and a woman was standing in front of the `Baby Belling' two-ring cooker with her back to the door. She was wearing a long orange shirt of silky material and baggy black shalwar, a thick plait of dark, gleaming hair hung down her back to her waist. In the deep pan on the cooker, onions and spices were sizzling as she stirred some vegetables into them and a hot mouth-watering smell caught Yasmin at the back of her throat as she opened the door. The woman swung round startled, and smiled warmly.

"Hi!" she said. "Do you want to use the cooker?" Yasmin noticed her long prominent nose, her smooth brown skin and her large eyes, circled with black kohl.

"No, I'm just getting my milk," she answered shyly, and made for the fridge. When she looked round the woman was peeling some potatoes, the orange and gold bangles piled on her arm tinkling gently as her thin fingers worked the small knife in rapid vigorous movements. Yasmin hesitated for a moment as she swung the fridge door shut, wondering if she should make further conversation.

"Well, I'll be going then," she said awkwardly.

"See you," the woman smiled, glancing up momentarily from her work.

Yasmin returned to her room with a lingering feeling of curiosity. When she slipped back through the door she found Trish standing by her desk, looking at the cards and photos on the large pinboard above the desk. She wondered if they thought it was wimpy of her to have a picture of her cat on the wall, or if they thought her posters boring.

"Is this your Mum and Dad?" Trish asked, squinting at a photo of two people hanging on to each other and laughing on a windswept mountainside.

"It's my Mum and Rod, her boyfriend. He's not my Dad," Yasmin explained briefly, looking up from the corner where she was pouring the tea. "That's when we were on holiday in Scotland."

"And is this you cycling in Scotland?" Trish asked, pointing to another photograph.

"No, that's out on the moors near our house in Sheffield."

"Have you always lived there?" Trish probed, as Yasmin handed her a mug of tea.

"Yes, since I was about four."

"So where do you come from, originally?"

Yasmin heard a little alarm bell ring somewhere in the back of her head at this question, but she shut it off firmly.

"London, I'm afraid," she smiled trying to look relaxed. "Very boring, I know."

"I just wondered," Trish murmured casually. "You don't look English, that's all. And with a name like Yasmin. You don't mind me asking, do you?"

"Of course not," Yasmin replied breezily, feeling the hot flush in her cheeks. She wondered why this conversation never got any easier however many times it happened. She searched momentarily for words that sounded right and eventually they came out in a self-conscious rush. "My mother's English, well half- English, half-Irish and my Dad's from Pakistan, but he's not with us any more. So I suppose I'm a mixture of English, Irish and Pakistani."

"How interesting!" Trish exclaimed. "I wish I had some exciting exotic ancestry! My family are all from Essex, we're really boring. We were trying to guess where you were from last night. I thought you might be Italian and Sharon said Arabian, so she was closer, wasn't she? What happened to your Dad, then?"

"Don't be so nosy, Trish," Sharon laughed awkwardly.

"I'm only asking," Trish retorted. "What's wrong with that?"

"It's all right," Yasmin interrupted, feeling intensely irritated at Trish's pretence of innocence. There was a slightly cold, challenging note underneath it which Yasmin recognised of old and bridled against immediately. She rarely thought about her father, except

13

at times like this, when she felt forced to explain herself in words that never expressed what she wanted, to people she felt instinctively would not understand. "He lives in Pakistan, that's all, and we live here, so we don't ever see him."

"That's like me," Sharon responded quickly, with a sympathetic glance. "My parents are divorced and my Dad works in Germany a lot so I hardly ever see him. I couldn't bear it if he didn't come over at least once a year though. It must be hard for you with your Dad so far away?"

"Not really," Yasmin replied. "I never knew him. I was only three when he left."

It was impossible to explain the confused, shadowy presence of this person in her life. The thought of him sparked a flare of carefully nurtured anger, which was entangled in old memories of a bleak, cold flat and the terror of seeing her mother cry. All she knew, or cared to know, was that he had left them and had upset her mother deeply. She had no clear memories of him herself, only a dim picture of her mother and a man in a big heavy coat hugging by the front door of their first flat. A cold wind was blowing rain in through the open doorway. Her mother seemed to be swallowed up in the big coat and she felt frightened and shut out. It was not a happy memory.

There were a few old black and white photographs too, but no-one ever looked at them. Her mother had shown them to her once when she had asked what her father looked like. He was young and dashing in the photos, his arm round her mother's waist as they posed by a fountain, or standing stiffly by a stone arched doorway, which her mother said was in his college in London. He had dark oiled hair, parted on one side and combed back, and a small, neat moustache, and his face was round and boyish. Yasmin had recognised with a shock her own soft, childish features and her wide mouth and dark eyes. There was one photo of him holding her as a baby, enveloped in a white shawl with her tiny face peeping out. And another of all three of them, having a picnic on an old blanket, she was reaching her chubby arms out to both of them and they were smiling and laughing at her. This last photo she kept with her, in an Indian lacquered jewellery box her mother had bought for her one Christmas, where she also kept photos of her Gran and an assortment of chains and necklaces she had worn in her early teens, most of which were now broken or discoloured. She was not sure why she kept the photo, she rarely looked in the box, but she always knew where it was and kept it safely hidden away in a drawer or a suitcase.

Yasmin realised the conversation had moved on and Sharon was telling Trish about going to Forces' schools in Germany when she was a child.

"My dream was to just live in one place!" Sharon explained. "You think it's boring because you've lived in the same house all your life, but to me that's like heaven. We were always moving, or if we weren't then my best friend at the time, she'd move, and that was just as bad. That was until my Mum left my Dad and took us all to Bristol, after that we stayed put, thank goodness."

Yasmin wondered if Sharon's mother was still on her own or had got involved with someone else, but she didn't like to ask.

"Hey, Yaz," Trish broke into Yasmin's thoughts. "Is there any tea left in the pot?"

"Oh, yes, pass us your mug," Yasmin replied, lifting the teapot lid to check what was left. "I hope it's still hot."

"She was miles away," Sharon laughed. "Penny for your thoughts, Yasmin?"

"I was thinking about tomorrow," Yasmin improvised quickly. "What did you think of Miss Mellor?"

"She doesn't half pile on the reading," Sharon replied. "You'd think they'd let us get used to things first, we can't spend all week in the library."

"They don't really expect you to read all that," Trish consoled her. "They just want to scare you into doing some work, my brother says no-one pays any attention to reading lists."

Yasmin was getting tired of hearing about Trish's brother, but she hoped they wouldn't notice she had actually pinned her reading list on her pinboard, along with the selection of photos and `arty' postcards transferred from her room at home.

"I want to go into town after lectures tomorrow," Sharon said. "Do either of you want to come? I've got loads of things to buy, as long as my grant comes through."

"I will," Yasmin volunteered eagerly. "I've thought of lots more things too. I thought I'd got everything when I left home, but as soon as you get here you find there's loads you've forgotten, don't you?"

"Yeah, like I brought all these posters and no Blutac!" Trish laughed. "That's how I found out Sharon was in the room next door."

"There I was, minding my own business," Sharon continued the story, "cutting my toenails at eleven o'clock at night, and this madwoman appears at the door, brandishing weird posters and asking for BLUTAC! I ask you! She kept me up 'till two o'clock in the morning, putting up those posters, they took forever. Should the poppies go over the bed? Would Tom Cruise be too distracting over the desk? You should have seen it!"

Yasmin watched as they collapsed into helpless laughter over their own private joke. Their closeness reminded her of Jenny, and listening to tapes in the cramped room Jenny shared with her sister, laughing 'till it hurt over things only they understood. She must write to Jenny soon, she thought, she had promised she would.

"You coming tomorrow, Trish?" Sharon asked, when she had recovered. "You could get your own Blutac and biscuits and nail varnish remover."

"No thanks, I'd rather use yours!" Trish replied, winking at Yasmin.

"Suit yourself," Sharon said, happily. "We'll have a good time," and she smiled conspiratorially at Yasmin.

"God, Sharon, look at the time!" Trish cried out suddenly, looking at her watch. "We said we'd meet Fiona and Ruth and the rest at half-five."

"We're going to a pizza place in town for something to eat," Sharon explained. "Do you want to come?"

"No thanks," Yasmin replied, not quite sure why she was saying no, but she knew she had to finish her letter and she didn't feel like going out with a big crowd.

"Sure?" Sharon asked, her eyebrows lifted in inquiring concern.

"Yeah, I've got some letters to write and I don't like pizza," Yasmin explained, not wanting Sharon to feel sorry for her.

"We could always go for a curry, if you'd rather," Trish offered, rising from the low chair and picking up her jacket. Yasmin cast a quick suspicious glance in her direction, but could not see the expression on Trish's face. She felt hot anger seething within her, but bit her tongue and let it pass.

"Oh no," she insisted shortly. "I don't eat a lot of curries either."

"Okay, well we'll see you tomorrow at the linguistics lecture then," Sharon said, getting up too. "Thanks for the tea. Sorry we've scoffed all your biscuits!"

"No problem," Yasmin laughed, following them to the door. "Thanks for popping round and have a good meal tonight."

She watched them for a moment as they walked off down the corridor, bickering about how late they were, then she closed the door and strolled thoughtfully across the room to her desk, her head buzzing with things to fill her letter with. She glanced happily at the emptied mugs and scattering of biscuit crumbs on the floor, switched her radio on to the Sunday afternoon chart show and began writing again.

2

CORRIDOR CONNECTION

By the time Yasmin went out to post her letter, the sun had sunk behind the trees and swathes of pink cloud streaked the golden sky to the west. She wheeled her bike out from the bicycle sheds at the back of the hall and pushed herself off down the tarmac drive, swinging one leg over the back wheel and settling onto the hard seat with practised ease. The cold wind tingled her face and ruffled through her thick wavy hair, blowing dark strands across her face. Her skin was the colour of caramel, a warm golden brown, and she had soft open features, with a small nose and a wide smiling mouth. There were faint shadows around her dark brown eyes which sometimes gave her a slightly weary, serious air. She cycled in long, easy revolutions, gliding smoothly through affluent tree-lined avenues with tidy gardens full of late roses and large cars parked up on immaculate paved drives. She felt a sense of lightness and release at being away from the cramped rooms and neon-lit corridors of her hall for a while.

After posting her letter, she returned along the quiet lane behind the halls. The air smelt of damp earth and leaves, and muffled animal rustles could be heard in the copse over the wall. Beneath the dark overhanging trees there was an autumn chill that reminded her of countless afternoons walking home from school at dusk, kicking up piles of dead leaves along the pavement by the cemetery wall. Turning through the gate into the grounds of the hall, she felt a small thrill of triumph as she realised afresh that she was actually here, at last, after so many months of suspense and uncertainty. The massive grey edifice before her was home and she felt a warm solidarity at the thought of the hundreds of conversations happening beyond the glowing patchwork of orange and red-curtained windows.

She parked her bike in the gloomy shed and walked round to the front of the hall. As she skirted the lawns in the dimming light, she noticed a young woman in an orange shirt and black shalwar approaching the hall from another direction. Yasmin recognised her as the student who had been in the kitchen earlier, she was carrying a pile of books and seemed in a hurry. She reached the big double doors to the hall ahead of Yasmin and scarcely glanced up as she hurried through. Inside Yasmin could see no sign of her and supposed she must have gone up some other staircase. She felt a little frustrated and wished she had called out, she wanted to know which room the woman lived in. She herself took the main stairs up to the first landing, where she turned off through the heavy fire doors onto her own corridor. It was steeped in its usual silence apart from the buzz of a faulty strip light near the bathroom. As she dug in her pocket for her key, the doors at the far end creaked open and she looked up to see the woman in the orange shirt shouldering her way through, balancing her books on one arm and steadying a door with the other. Yasmin moved to help her, but she was already through and smiled, saying, "Hello, I thought I'd seen you before! It was in the kitchen, wasn't it? I'm Rukhsana." She waited expectantly.

"Oh, I'm Yasmin," Yasmin replied, warmly, smiling with pleasure at having encountered her after all.

Rukhsana raised her eyebrows very slightly and fumbled in the bag slung over her shoulder. "Great to meet you, Yasmin, come in and have a drink. If I can find my keys. Here, can you hold these?" She held out her books and Yasmin grabbed the unruly pile, whilst Rukhsana rummaged amongst scraps of paper and a variety of eyebrow pencils, biros and hair brushes entwined with long dark hairs and ancient fluff. The keys were found in the bottom of the bag and Rukhsana let Yasmin into her room, which on first impressions, was not dissimilar to her bag, being dark, untidy and littered with fascinating objects. Rukhsana gestured to Yasmin to dump the books on the desk, which was already buried in cardboard files and loose papers, while she switched on the black angle-poise desk lamp and closed the curtains.

The lamp shed a grey, oblique light across the room, casting long shadows into the further recesses, where discarded clothing draped the floor in a tide of rich colours and textures. By the window seat there was a large red floor cushion and on the wall above the bed hung a printed cotton bedspread with an intricate crimson and turquoise pattern on a buff background. In the middle of the floor there was a long green and red cotton dhurrie with arrow and diamond patterns woven across it.

"Sorry about the mess," Rukhsana apologised cheerfully. "You can sit on the bed, just throw all that stuff over here. Tea or coffee?"

"Tea, please," Yasmin replied, settling herself on the bed, which had a faint lingering musty smell of sleep and rumpled bedclothes.

"You're a first year, aren't you?" Rukhsana sat on the floor cushion while she waited for the kettle to boil and idly fingered the end of her plait while she talked. "I'm doing finals this year, I was supposed to do all this work in the summer and I never did half of it, so I've been trying to catch up this week. I've just borrowed all those books from my mate 'cos I couldn't get them at home, the libraries there are crap and it's too much hassle to go all the way into London."

"Are you doing Physics?" Yasmin asked, having noticed the pages of scribbled formulae on the desk.

"Maths," Rukhsana corrected. "What about you?"

"French and Linguistics. I hated Maths at school, our teachers were really horrible and I never understood what I was doing."

"It's only like another language, really. I like it. Anyway, let's not talk about work, I'm sick of it. How are you getting on here? I was so miserable when I first came, I cried myself to sleep every night for the first month!"

"It's getting better," Yasmin laughed, encouraged by Rukhsana's openness. "It's a bit up and down, isn't it? I loved it the first couple of days. Yesterday I felt terrible, but I had some friends round today and I'm going to town with one of them tomorrow, so I'm beginning to feel more at home."

"Good. Well, you can knock on my door any time you feel lonely. I can always do with an excuse to stop work! I'll introduce you to some of the others on the corridor sometime, they're mostly quite human."

Rukhsana handed her a mug of tea and they sipped in silence for a few moments. Rukhsana was staring abstractedly at a point under the desk, lost in thought.

"I hope I'm not stopping you working," Yasmin said anxiously.

"No, not at all," Rukhsana looked up quickly. "Just ignore me, I'm always a bit spaced out when I've been working all day. I don't think my brain was made for this, and it's worse if you haven't done it for a while. We were so busy at home all summer, my sister got married a few weeks ago and all these visitors came. You know what it's like."

Yasmin murmured in agreement, though she had no idea what it was like.

"Have you just got one sister?" she asked.

"God, no! There are six of us," Rukhsana laughed. "Four girls and two boys. The sister that got married was the eldest and I'm next, unfortunately. How many brothers and sisters have you got?"

"None," Yasmin replied.

Rukhsana looked surprised and put her mug down. "None at all? That's incredible! Must be peaceful in your house, you can't hear yourself think in ours!"

"It's all right," Yasmin said thoughtfully. "People always say that, but I'd have quite liked a sister, I think. Sometimes my Mum seems like a sister because there was only the two of us when I was little."

"Did your Dad die, then?" Rukhsana asked, looking concerned.

"No, he went back to Pakistan when I was little," Yasmin sighed. `Why is everyone so obsessed with him?' she thought irritably.

"So don't you ever see him?" Rukhsana asked, her dismay deepening.

"No, never," Yasmin replied, almost triumphantly. "But I know he's not dead. One of his friends promised my Mum he'd tell her if anything like that ever happened."

"Is your Mum from Pakistan as well?"

"No, she's English."

"Oh? So how did she meet him?"

"When he was at college," Yasmin explained. "She was a secretary in the college. They were together all through his course and he got a job after, but his Father died and he had to go home. We never heard from him after that."

"Did your Mum become a Muslim, then, when they got married?"

"Actually, they didn't get married. I suppose you think that's awful?" Yasmin looked across at Rukhsana defiantly, but Rukhsana shook her head, smiling.

"'Course I don't," she said. "I think it's dead romantic, falling in love with the college secretary, it's like a story from an Indian film. I'm sorry he left, though. Do you think you'll ever go to Pakistan to see him?"

"Oh no!" Yasmin replied vehemently. She didn't know how to explain to Rukhsana the absurdity of such a suggestion without being rude. They had no contact with Pakistan and there was no reason why she should ever want to see the man who had deserted her mother.

"I was born over there," Rukhsana said. "But I've never been back since we came and I was only seven then. I'd really like to go, it sounds so beautiful. My cousins went and they loved it. I know my Mum and Dad would really like to go, but they can't afford it with all us lot to look after. I keep thinking if I get a good job after I finish, I could save up and take them back as a treat, but then they give me a hard time and I don't feel like bothering!"

"What are you going to do when you finish?" Yasmin asked.

"Good question," Rukhsana replied, gloomily. "At the moment I haven't a clue. I'd be happy to stay on here another three years, but I'm not good enough. All I know is I'm not going to be an accountant or a maths teacher!"

"I know what you mean," Yasmin laughed. "I'd do anything rather than be a teacher!"

"Well, you don't have to even think about it for four years if you're doing French. You get a year abroad, don't you?"

"I know. It's the best thing about the course, I'm really looking forward to it and you don't just have to go to France either. You can go anywhere where they speak French, like West Africa or the Caribbean."

"You'll certainly change people's ideas of the typical English student!" Rukhsana laughed, and then seeing Yasmin's puzzled look, "I mean, you being Asian, they won't be expecting someone like you, will they?"

"Oh, I see," Yasmin replied awkwardly, feeling very confused, and not knowing how to respond. "I don't know if they'll be expecting anything in particular. Anyway, as long as I can teach a bit of English I don't suppose it'll matter, will it?"

"Not if you don't think so," Rukhsana said evenly, leaning across to switch her kettle on again. Then she looked up as a new idea flashed across her face. "Listen, are you hungry?"

"Fairly," Yasmin replied.

"I've still got plenty of food left from this afternoon, aloo gobi. How do you fancy some?"

"Are you sure there's enough?" Yasmin asked cautiously.

"Course there is! You do know what aloo gobi is, don't you?"

"Well, actually, no," Yasmin confessed, smiling ruefully. Rukhsana laughed and said consolingly, "Never mind. You'll soon learn a bit of Punjabi if you hang around me, especially if you're a linguist! It's potato and cauliflower. Is that okay? Good, let's go and heat it up, we can have it with pittas. It's impossible trying to make rotis in this place, they haven't even got any gas cookers."

Yasmin followed Rukhsana down the corridor to the

kitchen and was put in charge of watching the pitta bread in the toaster.

"Not ideal, but what can you do without a proper grill?" Rukhsana confided. When the pittas popped out, steaming hot and soft, Yasmin wrapped them quickly in a tea towel, as instructed.

"Did your father speak Punjabi?" Rukhsana asked as she stirred the curry with a large wooden spoon.

"I don't know," Yasmin replied, trying to remember the little she had been told.

"Well, where was he from in Pakistan?"

"Lahore, I think."

"That's near where I'm from!" Rukhsana exclaimed excitedly. "I bet he spoke Punjabi, then. He never taught you any?"

"No, I was only three when he left and I think they always spoke English. I don't think my Mum speaks any of his language, but then I suppose I never asked her."

"What about your friends at school?"

"Oh, they were all English. There was hardly anybody else, you know. And they weren't in my class."

She remembered with a feeling of shame and confusion the black pupils who came on a special school bus from the high-rise flats down in the valley. Her own friends had said awful things about them that she knew she should argue with, her Mum would expect her to, but she had just changed the subject and tried to pretend it wasn't happening. She remembered a Vietnamese boy in the class next to hers, who was called John and had been adopted. She didn't remember there being any Indian or Pakistani children at all, certainly not in her year.

"You must feel like you missed out on your Dad's culture," Rukhsana said, commiserating with Yasmin.

Yasmin shrugged her shoulders with a gesture of indifference, and replied, "Not really. What use would it be? I'm not interested in all that stuff about family history and family trees and everything. One of my uncles is obsessed with it, he reckons he can trace our family right back to some Scottish laird hundreds of years ago. I think it's daft, I like to live in the present and I grew up here with my Mum, didn't I? My Mum says family are more of a burden than a help anyway, you shouldn't have to like them just 'cos they're blood relations. Her family were awful to her over my Dad."

"I bet they were," Rukhsana said with feeling. "I think this is ready now. That'll be enough pittas. Can you pass me the dishes?"

Rukhsana spooned the curry out into bowls and they carried the bowls, the wrapped pittas, and a carton of orange juice, back to Rukhsana's room, where Yasmin sat on the floor cushion and Rukhsana sat cross-legged on the cotton dhurrie, her bowl on the floor before her. Yasmin watched her tearing pieces off her pitta bread and scooping up mouthfuls of thick pulpy curry with unconscious ease. She had never eaten curry like this herself, they always had it with rice at home, and she felt a bit helpless without a spoon, but she followed Rukhsana's lead carefully and found it was easy enough to work out as she went along.

"It's delicious," she told Rukhsana, licking the sauce off her fingers. "Do you enjoy cooking?"

"Hate it!" Rukhsana laughed. "But I hate the meals in hall even more. We're not really supposed to cook proper meals up here, it's just supposed to be for snacks, otherwise they wouldn't make enough money out of us. But I have to have vegetarian because they don't do halal meat. I wouldn't mind that, only they've no idea how to cook interesting vegetarian meals. It's all omelettes and cheese pies and they don't use any spices, it's so boring. Do you know about halal meat?"

"'Fraid not," Yasmin confessed. "I really don't know anything about Pakistan."

"Well, it's more about being a Muslim, actually," Rukhsana explained. "Our meat has to be slaughtered a special way, otherwise we believe it's not clean. Also, we don't eat any pork because we believe pigs are unclean. It's easier just to be a vegetarian when I'm away from home."

"We're vegetarians," Yasmin said. "It was a right bother when I was at junior school, 'till they started letting us take packed lunches."

Rukhsana wiped round her plate with a last piece of bread and lifted herself from her seated position in a single flowing movement.

"What sort of music do you like?" she asked, walking over to the record player. "I've got reggae, soul, bhangra, songs in Urdu, classical... you name it!"

"Oh, anything," Yasmin laughed. "There's too much choice. You choose."

Rukhsana took a record out of its sleeve with great care and put it on the turntable. Her records and tapes were obviously her most valued possessions as they were neatly stacked in smart black plastic record and tape cases in the corner by the desk and looked a sizeable collection. The record began with a haunting melody on a stringed instrument, then a complicated beat was struck up on a small drum and a woman's voice began singing very sweetly and rhythmically in an Asian language.

"Is this in Urdu?" Yasmin asked.

"Yes. She's called Najma. I play this all the time because I just love her voice and the words are good too. When there's no-one here I sing along."

"I love singing too," Yasmin interrupted, enthusiastically. "I was in the choir at school and I was thinking of getting into a choir here, but there are so many things to get involved in I feel like I ought to do something new. Freshers' Fair was unbelievable, there are so many societies to choose from, it's really exciting."

"What are you interested in?" Rukhsana prompted.

"Well, there are the choirs, like I said, and there's a French Film Society, which would be good for my course, I suppose. Then there's loads of voluntary work, like visiting old people and stuff. When I was in the sixth form my best friend and I used to help out once a week in a youth club for children with learning difficulties. I really enjoyed it, Jenny's still going, she says they're all asking when I'm coming back, I quite miss it really."

"So why not do something like that here?"

"I think I will. What do you do?"

"I go to very different things now from what I did in the first year," Rukhsana began. "I did a lot of drama at first, but I got pissed off because I never got the parts I wanted. You know, at school we were nearly all Asian so we could be whatever part we wanted, it was great. But here they want you to `look the part', which means whatever you look like to them. I ended up always being the maid with two lines or something, I hated it. I used to play badminton as well, I haven't played that for ages. Now I do more things out of the university. I do some sessions in a Citizens' Advice Bureau and I help out at the Law Centre, interpreting for people who speak Punjabi and Urdu. We've also got an Asian Students' Society in the university, you'll have to come along sometime."

"Mmm," Yasmin responded non-committally. `I couldn't go to anything like that,' she thought to herself, `how do I explain to her? She doesn't seem to understand.' "Look, I'd better go, you've got loads to do. Thanks ever so much for the tea."

"Oh, don't worry about me, I work best between the hours of midnight and five a.m.!" Rukhsana reassured her. "Stay as long as you like."

"No, really," Yasmin insisted. "I must go, I've got things to do too. Thanks. The music's great, by the way."

"Do you like it? I'll do you a tape, with some other Urdu songs on the back," Rukhsana offered, as she followed Yasmin to the door.

Yasmin hesitated in the corridor, searching for a way of extending this new and fascinating contact. "Thanks. Why don't you come across later for a drink if you want a break from your work?" she invited, turning back as she left the room.

Rukhsana smiled warmly in agreement and said, "Good idea. I will. See you later." She closed the door gently.

3
UNIVERSITY LIVES

It was a warm, mellow October and the sun shone day after day on the golden lime trees and smooth-trunked beeches, as they shed flurries of burnished leaves over the pavements. After breakfast in hall, Yasmin would walk briskly into the university, across the wide blustery expanses of a nearby park and through quiet terraced streets, joining the converging, swelling stream of students all heading the same way. Sometimes she would meet up with Sharon and Trish, sometimes with other students from her course.

Occasionally Rukhsana was up in time and felt like a walk, but more usually she missed breakfast and dashed out for a bus at the last moment.

Rukhsana could not understand how Yasmin liked having breakfast with two hundred other people, it was her own worst nightmare.

Yasmin liked the sociability of discussing the coming day with her friends over thin slices of buttered toast and stewed tea from a large stainless steel urn. She enjoyed the fact that she never knew who would be in for breakfast and there would be a moment, after emerging from the self-service counter balancing a tray, when she would look around for a familiar face to sit next to. Catching sight of such faces was always a pleasure and she would hurry over to the table to be warmly welcomed into low-key companionable chatter as they all eased themselves into the day. Sometimes, if there was no-one she knew particularly well, she would sit alone and watch with amusement the stream of dazed and bleary-eyed faces shuffling down the queue.

After breakfast Yasmin would go back to her room for her jacket and rucksack of books and files, and then she would set off for the Modern Languages Faculty, which was housed in a grand Victorian terrace leading off from the main university buildings. Her seminars and classes were held in the comfortable intimate rooms of these old houses with their elaborate plastered mouldings and wide bay windows looking out onto the leafy square. Lectures were in the Arts Block, a multi-storey building of concrete and glass with cavernous lecture halls in its basement. Between lectures, conversation classes and seminars on French culture and politics, there was plenty of time to spend in the students' union coffee bar or visiting friends' rooms for afternoon tea.

The days seemed to glide by effortlessly and there was always plenty to do in the evenings, parties, films in the union, meeting people in the pub, the youth club Yasmin had started helping out with once a week, or just listening to music in each others' rooms. Academic work had to be fitted around this social whirl and Yasmin increasingly found herself joining Rukhsana in all-night essay-writing marathons in order to get work in on time. She rather enjoyed these sessions, there was something very special about being awake in the early hours of the morning when the rest of the world was asleep. If she opened her window onto the dark, hushed night, she could hear the distant hum of the city as she never noticed it in the day, a formless, ceaseless murmur with occasional bursts of sound, a dog barking, a car accelerating, a siren screaming far away. At these times she loved the silence in her room and the slightly high, light-headed feeling that came with lack of sleep. Essays written at night, in the white-hot concentration born of panic, were usually described by her tutors as, `fascinating' and `original, but disorganised', whereas essays written in the library through patient slogging were, `cogently argued' and `well-presented'. Her tutors, she knew, preferred the latter, but she thought the former much more fun to write and to read.

When Rukhsana was working the same night, they would take it in turns to make cups of tea and toast at agreed intervals, and would keep each other going with encouraging noises about the amount of paper covered,

29

although neither understood what the other was doing. Yasmin soon grew to recognise the sound of Rukhsana's door opening down the corridor, it was the same door she had heard voices disappear behind on that first Sunday, when she had envied them their confidence. Now she was almost as familiar with Rukhsana's room as she was with her own. She knew the soft jingle of bangles accompanying the tap on the door meant it was time for a break. She would retire to her window seat, wrapping her red dressing gown around her, while Rukhsana sat on the bed in a loose green shalwar kameez that she kept for lounging about in her room. They would both sip hot reviving tea and commiserate with each other over how much there was still left to do, in an atmosphere buzzing with intellectual energy and gentle intimacy.

They rarely saw each other during the day, but would invariably meet when they returned to their rooms in the evening. Sometimes Yasmin would eat with Rukhsana rather than go downstairs for dinner in hall, as Rukhsana persisted in flouting all the rules and cooking elaborate meals on the two electric rings in the kitchen. Yasmin would contribute a salad or a dessert and they would eat in Rukhsana's room, sitting on the rug or on cushions and drinking mango juice in Rukhsana's best mugs.

Yasmin first met Rukhsana's friends at such a meal. They had just settled down to eat when there was a knock at the door and they both looked up as the door swung open and two young Asian women swept into the room.

"Hiya, Rukhsana. Mmm, that smells good! Any left for us?"

"Too late, my dear," Rukhsana laughed. "Meet Yasmin. Yasmin, this is Shahnaz and Atiya. Get yourselves some mugs and you can have some juice."

Shahnaz and Atiya smiled curiously at Yasmin, as she gestured hello to them with her mug.

"Rukhsana's told us all about you," Atiya winked mischievously, perching on the end of the bed. She was dressed in smart jeans and a white polo shirt underneath a black jacket, large silver earrings dangled against her black hair, which was cut in a short stylish bob. She seemed older than the rest of them and very self-assured. "You've got a room on this corridor, haven't you? Rukhsana says you're as bad as her, always leaving your work 'till the middle of the night!"

"Well thanks, Rukhsana!" Yasmin laughed, lifting her eyebrows at Rukhsana in mock surprise.

"You're welcome," Rukhsana replied nonchalantly.

"Atiya's a medic so she doesn't understand what real work is, of course, they just play around with bones all day. Hey! Watch my food!" Atiya motioned to throw a pillow at Rukhsana, but stopped at the last minute.

"Doesn't that take forever, medicine?" Yasmin asked.

"Feels like it," Atiya replied sighing. "Six years of exams, I must be mad."

"She loves it really," Shahnaz confided, from the window seat, where she was quietly sipping her drink and watching Yasmin. She had a strong Scottish accent which caught Yasmin by surprise, and a studious air which probably came from her small, wire-rimmed glasses.

"What do you think of the place so far?" Atiya asked Yasmin.

"Oh, it's great," Yasmin replied enthusiastically. "I've never been out so much or had so much fun and I've made loads of friends."

"Been homesick yet?"

"A bit the first few days, but now I hardly think about it, I'm too busy. I was going to go home next weekend, actually, but I changed it to the one after as there's a disco on Friday and a pyjama jump on Saturday."

"Oh God, not a pyjama jump!" Shahnaz cried out in horror. "They're vile! Honestly, all those revolting drunken men in nightdresses, you've never seen anything so disgusting!"

Yasmin looked slightly taken aback and Rukhsana leapt in to defend her. "Don't be like that, Shahnaz, I bet you went in the first year. It's all right just the once."

"It'll be an experience," Yasmin said cheerfully. "I'll tell you what I think afterwards."

"So, did you have a good time on Saturday, Atiya?" Rukhsana asked, turning to Atiya with a teasing smile.

"Very nice, thank you," Atiya replied primly, pretending to flick a piece of fluff off her jacket. Shahnaz and Rukhsana burst out laughing and Atiya smiled indulgently.

"Atiya's in love," Rukhsana explained to Yasmin.

"They can't keep away from each other, it's just too romantic!"

"And you're not, I suppose?" Atiya retaliated indignantly. "Or have we forgotten a certain Vikram who just happens to agree with everything you say at Asian Soc.?"

Rukhsana flushed deeply and forced a laugh. "Don't be silly, he's always arguing with me," she said quickly. "We're just mates, there's nothing going on."

"Have it your way," Atiya said soothingly, "Anyway, that's what we came to say, how about coming to our house this Wednesday after the meeting? You could stay the night and you wouldn't have to leave so early, we could get a cab back to Sharwood all together."

"Great," Rukhsana replied. "Thanks, I'll do that."

"Well, time to get back to work," Shahnaz said decisively. "Thanks for the drink. We'll leave you to eat in peace."

Rukhsana got up and showed them to the door, where they stood talking for a while longer, making arrangements for later on in the week. When they had gone, she returned to her cushion, looking preoccupied, and said, almost to herself, "I hope Atiya keeps her big mouth shut to Vikram, I'll die if she says anything to him."

"Who is he?" Yasmin asked.

"Oh, he's just someone in the Asian Soc. Remember I was telling you we've got an Asian Students' Society? And I've fancied him for ages, but I don't think he knows and I never told anyone 'till I made the stupid mistake of telling Atiya. If she sticks her nose in he might just back right off and then I'll die of embarrassment and I won't see him at all." Rukhsana looked dismayed at this prospect.

"Can't you tell her you fancy someone else? Then she'll forget about Vikran."

"Vikram," Rukhsana corrected her. "I suppose I could, but I don't think she'd believe me. Anyway, I'm stupid to like him. We've only got a few months left and then we'll both be leaving and going our different ways. He's not even a Muslim, it's just silly."

"It doesn't sound silly to me," Yasmin said, trying to reassure her. "Surely Atiya won't spoil things for you if she's your friend?"

"You don't know Atiya, she's such a stirrer," Rukhsana replied. "Anyway, there's no point worrying about it."

After that, Yasmin met Atiya and Shahnaz quite often in Rukhsana's room, along with two other women called Manjula and Asha, who were also both finalists. She enjoyed meeting them and liked the way they always included her in the conversation, as if it were quite natural that she should be there, even though she was a first year and she often felt quite different from them. She preferred to be on her own with Rukhsana and occasionally felt a stab of disappointment if she and Rukhsana were already engrossed in conversation and the others turned up. But she also liked to be in company with Rukhsana, watching her easy laughter and teasing wit weave a strand of brilliance into the fabric of the gathering. Sometimes Rukhsana would invite her out with them, but Yasmin was usually too busy, or not sure she was interested in what they were doing. Also, she felt slightly embarrassed because she never invited Rukhsana out with her friends. She told herself Rukhsana would find it boring to go out with a load of first years.

It was easy to keep her friendship with Rukhsana very separate from her other friendships, it was almost as if she led two lives, one with her first year friends from her course and from the hall where Sharon and Trish lived, and another life back at `home', on her own corridor, with

Rukhsana and her friends. She found herself changing and moderating as she moved from one world to the other. She moved differently, talked differently, even dressed differently, according to who she was spending time with.

She was particularly fascinated by Rukhsana's clothes and the ease with which she switched from flowing shalwar kameez one day to trousers and long shirts or sweaters the next, and often mixed the two as she had done on the first day Yasmin met her. Yasmin had never known anyone whose clothes were such a dramatic and vivid expression of herself and the many sides of her life. Rukhsana encouraged Yasmin to try her clothes and to borrow them if she wanted, she had even given Yasmin a couple of tops she hardly wore herself, a maroon shirt with a faint squiggly design, and a very loose black t-shirt. Yasmin wore the black t-shirt all the time, she felt confident and attractive in it, she had never realised before how well black suited her hair and skin colour. She also felt that maybe some of Rukhsana's style rubbed off on her, or even that she could imagine being Rukhsana when she wore it. She felt safe trying things on in Rukhsana's room, but she couldn't imagine ever wearing most of Rukhsana's clothes outside, or even when her other friends were around, she felt too shy, and wary of their reactions.

Trish and Sharon did not meet Rukhsana until the fourth week of term, and then it was by accident in the students' union coffee bar. Yasmin and Trish had just come out of a lecture on Medieval French Language and met up with Sharon for lunch. The coffee bar was a vast, low-roofed, airless room in the basement of the union building, with orange plastic seating and grey formica-topped tables. A permanent pall of cigarette smoke hung below the rectangular strip lights and the tables were littered with old coffee cups and empty crisp packets. A local commercial radio station was usually blaring through speakers on the walls and at lunchtime the whole area echoed with voices raised above the radio's background music. Yasmin hated the smoky air, but she loved the sociable buzz of conversation and the mugs of frothy hot chocolate that were a coffee bar speciality.

She and Trish found a table in one corner, while Sharon fetched their usual sandwiches and mugs of hot chocolate.

"I wish I could write as fast as you," Trish complained, dumping her bag heavily on the seat beside her. "He mumbles into his beard so you can hardly hear what he's saying. They should make all lecturers do a course in elocution, or public speaking or something, before they let them loose on us."

"I like him, he's quite funny, when you get used to his sense of humour," Yasmin commented. "It can't be easy trying to make mediaeval language interesting."

"Oh, you like everybody," Trish said crossly.

"No, I don't," Yasmin countered, feeling annoyed herself. "I don't like Mr. Hutchinson, I think he's a real creep, but most of the other lecturers are okay and I think Mr. Gray's nice, he says hello in the corridor. At least he remembers who we are."

Sharon arrived with a loaded tray, interrupting the conversation, and squeezed in next to Yasmin. The coffee bar was filling up fast for lunch and it was very hot and noisy.

"Mmm...I've been dying for a drink all morning," Sharon said sipping her chocolate. "So, have you two had a good morning?"

"Don't ask..." Yasmin began, and then she saw Rukhsana making her way down the aisle towards them, looking for an empty seat. For a moment Yasmin was not sure what to do and hesitated. Then Rukhsana spotted her and hurried over, smiling warmly in recognition.

"Hello, Yasmin, isn't it busy in here?" she said as she reached them, shaking back her hair, which she was wearing loose today, falling in a soft black curtain over her shoulders and back.

"Horrendous," Yasmin agreed. "Why don't you sit here, there's another seat?"

"Oh, yes, here you are," said Trish, moving her bag

quickly, and Rukhsana put her tray down on the table and slipped in beside her. Yasmin introduced them all and there was a slight pause as they let the din of the amplified radio wash over them and considered each other with interest. Yasmin felt a responsibility to fill the silence and she began explaining to Sharon and Trish, "Rukhsana lives in Ascombe Hall, she's just across the corridor from me."

"Oh?" Sharon interrupted surprised. "Yasmin! You never said you had a friend in hall."

"I'm sure I did," Yasmin replied blushing, and turning to Rukhsana, "We all do linguistics together, I think I told you about Trish and Sharon?"

"Yes, of course," Rukhsana smiled. "I hope you both enjoyed the pyjama jump as much as Yasmin did, she had a hell of a hangover on Sunday morning!"

"Oh God! Didn't we all!" Trish moaned. "I was in bed all day Sunday, I swore I'd never drink again, but that only lasted 'till Monday. Oh, I'm sorry! I don't suppose you drink, do you?"

"Don't I?" Rukhsana replied, stirring her tea and smiling politely.

"I thought it was against your religion?" Trish looked at her, innocently.

"I thought it was against all religions," Rukhsana scrunched up the plastic wrapper her sandwich had come in and dropped it in her plate. Then she turned away from Trish deliberately. Yasmin gave Trish a murderous glance and was about to say something, but Rukhsana had already begun to speak to her, saying, "How's this week's essay going, Yasmin?"

"Oh, not too bad," Yasmin replied, uncomfortably. "I want to finish it this afternoon 'cos we're going to see `Baghdad Cafe' here tonight. Otherwise, I'll have to do it when I get back from the film."

"Well I'll probably still be working then, I've got loads on today," Rukhsana sighed.

"I'll bring you a cup of tea when I get in," Yasmin promised.

"What do you do?" Sharon asked Rukhsana.

"Maths! For my sins."

"Oh, I did Maths for `A' level, Pure and Applied," Sharon responded enthusiastically and the two of them chatted for a while about Rukhsana's course.

Then Rukhsana gathered up her jacket and bags and rose from the table.

"I must go now. Nice meeting you," she nodded to Sharon and Trish. "See you tonight, Yasmin. Enjoy the film," and she made her way back down the busy aisle, soon merging with the crowd.

"You didn't tell us about her. I didn't know you'd made any friends on your corridor," Sharon insisted, turning to Yasmin when Rukhsana was out of sight.

"Well, I have," said Yasmin sharply. "I'm sure I must have mentioned her."

"She's Indian, isn't she?" Trish commented.

"Pakistani, actually."

"There was a girl called Rukhsana in my class at school," Trish continued. "She didn't mix with us much, none of them did. Know what I mean?"

"No! What do you mean?" Yasmin asked angrily. "You say the stupidest things sometimes, Trish!"

Trish turned to Sharon, undeterred, and continued stubbornly, "Well, I thought they were supposed to want to integrate, otherwise why did they bother coming here?"

"Maybe they tried, but people weren't very nice to them," Sharon suggested uneasily, looking anxiously at Yasmin. "You know what kids are like."

"Yes, but look at Yaz, she fits in with everything, don't you, Yaz? Those girls at school, they just didn't want to know," Trish argued.

Yasmin ignored her pointedly and stared across the room, her seething mind unable to formulate the withering retort she needed.

"That's 'cos your Mum's English, isn't it?" Sharon said to Yasmin in a conciliatory tone. "So you're bound to be more English, aren't you?"

"Really?" Yasmin snapped. "Look, Rukhsana's very friendly, she's really made me feel at home in hall."

"I don't think she liked us much," Trish said sullenly.

"Well, you did have to go and say something stupid about her religion," Sharon said. "What do you expect?"

"It wasn't stupid," Trish denied. "I was trying not to offend her, it's not my fault she took it the wrong way."

"She didn't take anything any way," Yasmin insisted hotly. "She came and had a chat with us, so what's the problem?"

"No problem," Sharon intervened. "I thought she was really nice. I hope we get to see her again, don't you Trish?"

"Yeah," Trish responded without enthusiasm.

"We'd better get moving, anyway. We've got essays to finish before tonight. Hope the film's worth all this rush."

They walked back across to the Arts block together, talking about work and their plans for the evening. Yasmin was relieved to reach the hushed seclusion of the Modern Languages library and find a space for herself in a corner of the study area. She laid her notes out on the table, alongside the text in French and a copy in translation, but she could not concentrate on the words before her. Her mind kept drifting back to the coffee bar conversation. She took out a blank sheet of paper and began writing a letter instead:

`Dear Mum,

I'm writing to you from the Modern Languages Library, which is five floors up in the Arts block. I'm supposed to be doing an essay, but I can't concentrate. It's really windy outside and I'm sure the whole building is moving! There's a lovely view of the city and all the parks and gardens with the trees in their autumn colours, it's very peaceful to look at.

I was going to phone you last night but there was such a queue by the phones and then when I got to a phone you were engaged, so here's a letter instead! Thanks for your lovely long letter, by the way. I'm glad you've finished the front room, I can't wait to see it. Hope you haven't been too busy at work this term - when I see how the Modern Languages secretary here is rushed off her feet, I always think of you.

I've been really busy these last couple of weeks, there's loads to do all the time and some of it's really hard, I can't bear to think what it'll be like in the third year. But I'm enjoying it as well and most of it's much more interesting than school. Rukhsana and I keep each other going when we have work to do late at night. She's really great, very kind and good fun, I'm sure you'd like her. I can't really describe what she's like, you'd have to meet her. Sometimes I think she's really my best friend, even though I see Sharon and Trish much more. She understands me really well and she's very clever. I'm glad now I ended up getting a room so late, I'd never have had the opportunity to meet her if I'd been on a corridor full of first years.

My wild social life gallops on out of control! Last week I went to a film on Tuesday, did the youth club on Thursday, went out for a drink on Friday with Sharon and her friend, Fiona, who does German with her (she's really nice), went to the pyjama jump on Saturday (which was just as sordid as I'd been warned, but good fun all the same) and to a birthday party last night in a house in town for one of Steve's friends. Steve is this bloke that Trish is going out with, he does Biology, and sometimes we all go out with him and his mates in a big crowd. It's great fun as long as Trish doesn't try to pair us off. I'm enjoying myself too much to be bothered with all that. People used to go on and on at school about who fancied who, it's nice to be out of it and be friends with blokes just on a sensible adult basis.

Last Tuesday I had to finish my essay after the film, so I was up 'till 4.30 in the morning, went to bed, and got up again at nine to take it in to my tutor! I'm heading that way this week as well, I'm afraid! Last night I didn't get back from the party 'till after two, and then I had to finish a translation, so today I'm shattered, with a whole essay still to do. But I had a really good time last night. Trish isn't always my favourite person, she can be quite rude and a bit selfish sometimes, but she's great fun at parties, she really knows how to have a good time and make everyone laugh.

I still like Sharon best of my course, she's easy to talk to and I think we've got a lot in common. Her parents are divorced and she was telling me her Mum's seeing another man - after years of not seeing anyone. Sharon doesn't seem to like him much and she worries about her younger brother and sister and what they feel. I told her how much I hated that Kevin you went out with, and how I wasn't very sure about Rod when you first met him, but it's great now and we all get on really well. I think she felt a bit better knowing someone else who'd been through it.

Sharon still sees her Dad once or twice a year. I've been thinking a bit about my Dad recently, since I met Rukhsana really. She says she's from the same area as him in Pakistan - if I remembered it right, it is Lahore, isn't it? - she speaks the same language as well. It got me wondering about him and why he never came back. Don't you wonder where he is and what he's doing? I know you're happy with Rod, but you must wonder sometimes. I suppose it's pointless, though, because we'll never know, will we?

I wrote to Jenny on Sunday, at last. I felt really bad, she's written me three letters since I've been here and I was just so busy, I kept meaning to write and didn't. Sounds like she's having a difficult time in the bank, she doesn't like the other people much and they're working her really hard. I suppose I felt a bit guilty having such a brilliant time and I didn't know what to say. Have you seen her at all? In her last letter she said her Mum was worse again, I wondered if you'd heard.

I'm looking forward to coming home at the weekend, I'll have been here a whole month by then! I can hardly believe it, the time's just flown, though in other ways I feel I've lived here for years, it's all so familiar now. The only thing I miss - apart from you and Rod and Tibby, of course! - is going walking. It's really difficult to get out into the country when you don't know anyone with a car and you don't know where's good to go anyway. I thought I might join the Rambling Club, but the people at Freshers' Fair looked such wallies and I haven't really got time. Never mind.

I go to a club on Thursday nights - like the one at Ash House that Jenny and I used to help at. The kids are great and we can take more responsibility for things ourselves, being students, I suppose. It makes me feel more ordinary and human going there once a week, takes me away from the university for a while and I remember there's a life outside! Rukhsana does a lot of stuff outside university as well. She helps in a C.A.B. and at the Law Centre, doing interpreting and giving advice in Punjabi and Urdu. She speaks five languages! I feel quite embarrassed, claiming to be a linguist when I only speak English and French, she speaks Punjabi, Urdu and English, she learnt Arabic at a mosque school and French at secondary school - impressive or what!

Must go now. I still haven't done my essay but I feel much more like it! Dying to see you next Friday - I'll get the train that arrives at 6.18 - don't worry about meeting me, I'll get a bus. Love to Rod. See you soon.

Tons of love,
Yasmin.'

4

CONFERENCE AT BREAKFAST

"23rd October: 1.00am

Met Rukhsana in the coffee bar today with Sharon and
Trish - bad news. It was really awkward because I hadn't
really said anything to them about Rukhsana. I don't
know why, it just seemed like she was nothing to do with
them and they never asked if I knew anyone on the
corridor so I never bothered to tell them. Rukhsana's
special somehow and I didn't want to mix her up with my
other friends, I don't know why. I suppose it got more and
more like having two different lives, I forgot that one day
they'd be bound to meet. Why don't I ever think ahead? I
felt so bad, Rukhsana knew I was lying when I tried to
cover up - she probably hates me now.

Trish was awful - just confirmed everything I've always
felt about her. I think she's really prejudiced. Of course
Rukhsana's very good at standing up for herself, but I felt
I should have said something - why am I so useless in
these situations? - I can never think fast enough and I
always feel guilty afterwards, when it's too late. - And
what did Sharon mean when she said I was different from
the girls at Trish's school because my Mum's English,
which makes me more English? Of course I'm different
from them, but it sounded like she was saying I was
different from her and Trish as well, like I'm more English,
but I'm not as English as them. Maybe she didn't mean it
like that, I just felt really odd when she said it, I thought
we were good friends.

I don't know what to do about Rukhsana now. I haven't
seen her since. She said she would be up working when I
got back tonight, but she's gone to sleep. I even turned the
light off in the corridor to check, but there's no light under
her door. There's nothing unusual in that, I suppose, but

42

she usually leaves me a note if she changes her mind about staying up. I can't help feeling she's fed up with me - I wouldn't blame her if she was. But I can't bear it if she's angry with me, I don't want her to think badly of me, she's too important. I hate everything being a mess, but that's what it feels like. I wish I could sort it out in my head. All I want is to be friends with Rukhsana and friends with Sharon and none of it be a problem. I hate all this bad feeling.

When I'm with Sharon and the others, I feel like I've always felt, just like at school with Jenny and Lisa, we're friends together, we're all the same, we speak the same language, eat the same food, listen to the same music, it feels like we're all British, whatever that means. Sometimes things come up that make me feel a bit different - like to do with my Dad or my name - but they're not important, they're just on the surface.

When I'm with Rukhsana I know we're different in lots of ways, but she makes me feel really at home and relaxed and I feel really close to her - if I'm honest, I feel much closer to her than to any of my other friends here. But surely that's just because she's such a wonderful person? She's got some great friends as well - I suppose they think of me as like them because of my name, and Rukhsana must have told them about my Dad. But I'm very different from them (they're quite different from each other too, actually) and sometimes I feel really out of it, even though they're so nice - like if they say something in their language or they're talking about Indian films.

Thinking about all this just gets me more confused - Mum always says nothing else matters as long as you're true to yourself and kind to other people, but how can you be true to your `self' if you're not sure who that is? I don't even know what to call myself, I never have done, that's why it's such a pain meeting new people. It doesn't seem to work just being myself, people still want to know `what' you are or where you come from and saying Sheffield never seems to satisfy them.

I hope my letter won't upset Mum, it's so long since I even mentioned my Dad. I only said a very little bit of what I've been thinking, just to give her an idea before I go home. I do want to talk to her, but I'm really scared about it, we've never talked about my Dad properly before, only in passing. There are lots of things I never thought of asking before I met Rukhsana. Now it seems really hard to ask them because so many years have gone by not saying anything. I suppose I avoided the subject because Mum gets so angry and upset - and I blame him too, for going off and leaving us, it seems like he didn't really care about us. Now I keep wondering where he is, and if he had other children. I might have brothers and sisters I don't even know about. He might even be in this country, not in Pakistan at all. I bet that Mr. Munir that Mum knows could find out if he wanted to. Maybe this is all stupid and pointless, but I keep thinking about it.

This isn't getting my essay written so I'd better stop. If I don't see Rukhsana in the morning, I'll be miserable all day, maybe I should wake her up after breakfast and we can talk before lectures. But she's always so grumpy first thing. - I hate not knowing what to do."

Rukhsana woke abruptly to the urgent electronic buzz of her alarm clock. Groaning, she reached for the button to silence it and then turned over, pulling the warm duvet back over her head. In the hot cocoon beneath the soft weight of the quilt she almost fell asleep again, but an uneasy feeling of something to be done stirred in the depths of her mind and lured her back to consciousness. What day was it? Oh yes, Wednesday, and yesterday she had met those friends of Yasmin's. That was what was wrong! She had to see Yasmin before she went to lectures or she might not see her 'till after the weekend. She was going to Asian Soc. tonight and staying the night at Atiya's, tomorrow night Yasmin would be out at her youth club, and then on Friday Yasmin was going home for the weekend. This feeling of unease she had with Yasmin had to be tackled now, it was too important to leave till after the weekend. Admittedly, last night she had wondered why she bothered and had gone to bed totally frustrated with Yasmin and herself. Even though it was was far too early to be doing anything as strenuous as getting up, Rukhsana persuaded herself it was in a good cause and flung off the covers in a heroic gesture.

Fifteen minutes later she was standing outside Yasmin's room in her dressing gown, banging on the door with her foot and supporting a tray of tea and toast in her arms.

"Hang on!" a voice croaked from within.

There was a hasty shuffling and fumbling with the lock and the door swung open. Yasmin and Rukhsana looked at each other in mutual astonishment for a moment. Yasmin was in her cotton striped pyjamas, her hair dishevelled from sleeping and her face sallow and tired, with dark shadows under her eyes. She looked slightly startled and even alarmed to see Rukhsana standing there.

"My God, you look how I feel!" Rukhsana laughed. "I've brought you breakfast, can I come in?"

"Of course," Yasmin stood back to let her pass and closed the door behind her. "But you never have breakfast."

"No, well, there's a first time for everything," Rukhsana replied. "Anyway, I wanted to see you before you disappeared for the weekend."

Yasmin sat down heavily on the bed.

"I'm really sorry about yesterday," she began looking anxiously across at Rukhsana. "I don't know why Trish was so stupid."

"I'm not bothered about her," Rukhsana interrupted firmly. "I'm bothered about you. Anyway, have some tea first, you look terrible, how late did you stay up?"

"I know, I'm sorry, I said I'd bring you some tea, didn't I? We went to get something to eat after the film, I didn't get back 'till about midnight and I finished my essay about five o'clock, I kept faffing around doing other things," she paused. "Are you cross with me?"

"Of course not," Rukhsana replied gently. "I just want to get one or two things straight, that's all."

Yasmin felt as if she were still asleep. She had been dreaming about something vaguely connected to the events the day before when she was woken by the knocking on her door. She tried hard to apply herself to the present conversation, but part of her mind was still searching for the lost thread of the dream. The tea was milky and comforting and she was surprisingly hungry considering she had eaten a whole packet of biscuits during the night.

"I must say I don't like your friend, Trish, you deserve better mates than her," Rukhsana began calmly, "but it's none of my business who else you go around with. What I want to know is why you never mentioned me, when you see me practically every day. Are you ashamed of being friends with me or what?"

"Of course not, that's ridiculous," Yasmin protested, indignantly, amazed that Rukhsana could have thought such a thing. "I just never thought to say anything, I don't know why. I knew you wouldn't get on with them. Anyway, we were always talking about other things, you know, work and where to go out and stuff."

"Sounds riveting. Look, Yasmin, I know there are lots of things you're trying to sort out. I've been there too, you know. I'm not asking you to have all the answers, I just don't want to be treated like some skeleton in a cupboard, or whatever the phrase is, know what I mean?"

Yasmin nodded quietly, she felt miserable and exhausted. She clamped her hands firmly round her mug as if hanging on to some lifeline.

"When I was waiting for you to come back last night," Rukhsana continued, "I thought about a few things. I didn't do my work because I got really angry. I felt like I was sitting around waiting for you as if you expected me to be there at the end of the day when you've finished seeing everyone else. So I decided I didn't want to be up when you came back. Anyway, what I thought was, if we're going to be friends, let's be proper friends, let's go out to things and make arrangements so you have to talk about me. You know, like, `sorry, I can't make that, I'm going to the pictures with Rukhsana on Friday'. Do you understand what I'm saying?"

"Yes, you're right," Yasmin agreed, wondering if this meant they were still friends.

"Hey, it's not that bad," Rukhsana coaxed cheerfully. "I'm not angry now, I just said that because I want things to be clear. What are you doing for lunch today?"

"I don't know," Yasmin replied, trying to remember what day it was. "I've got to take my essay in, and then there's a lecture at eleven I should go to, and after that I'm not doing anything, I don't think."

"Good," Rukhsana said. "Let's meet for lunch. What about that cafe in the art gallery? If you want to?"

"Oh yes, great idea," Yasmin enthused, realising that whatever was wrong was also redeemable.

"Half-past twelve?"

"Fine. I'm sorry I'm not very awake."

"I'm not surprised!" Rukhsana laughed, "I'd better leave you to get on with things. Don't worry about yesterday, it's not a problem any more. Okay? I'll see you at lunchtime, then."

After she had gone, Yasmin crept back into bed and, hiding her face in the pillow, let out a few long anguished sobs. Then she turned onto her back, sniffing miserably and groped around the small table for the tissue box. When she found a tissue she sat up and blew her nose vigorously. `I'm just overtired,' she thought, `it's going to be all right, if I can just get my act together. Anyway, it's not all my fault, if Trish wasn't such a difficult person, I might have introduced them all before. I knew she'd be like that, she just doesn't know how to keep her stupid, prejudiced thoughts to herself. She nearly lost me my best friend, I'm not going to get tangled up with her any more.'

She wondered what that would mean for her and Sharon. But Sharon had pulled Trish up on what she said, and she was a sensitive person, Yasmin told herself it would be okay. She felt exhausted by the demands being made on her to think about herself and where she stood between all these new people in her life. She wanted to tell someone who would understand, but there was no-one who would understand all the different bits put together, not her mother, not Jenny, not Sharon, not even Rukhsana who said she had `been there', but she couldn't have really because she must have always known who she was and what she thought about things.

Glancing at the travelling alarm clock by her bed, Yasmin realised she was late and leapt out of bed again, pushing these thoughts to the back of her mind as she concentrated on getting into the university for half-past nine.

The cafe was on the top floor of the art gallery and was airy and modern with black-and-white photographs of railings, pavement grates and other `street furniture' decorating the blank white walls. The round tables and red folding chairs were scattered unevenly to give the area a slightly disorganised appearance and a long counter displayed colourful salads, quiches and trays of succulent pastries. As she entered, Yasmin spotted Rukhsana sitting in the far corner, reading a paperback novel, with a small pot of tea in front of her. She looked up and waved and Yasmin felt a twinge of nerves and wondered if she would always feel like this now, precarious and as if everything was different from before. She joined the short queue at the counter and bought an egg mayonnaise sandwich and another pot of tea and carried them over to Rukhsana's table.

"Hi, aren't you having anything to eat?" she asked Rukhsana as she unloaded her tray.

"I was here early so I've already had a sandwich," Rukhsana explained putting her book down on the table. "I've been mega-efficient today, it's done me wonders getting up so early, I'll have to do it more often!"

Yasmin poured herself a cup of tea. Rukhsana was twisting the hair at the end of her plait in a familiar unconscious gesture, and looking quizzically at Yasmin from beneath her heavy eyelids. Yasmin felt strangely shy, as if they were meeting for the first time again.

"Did you get your essay in on time?" Rukhsana asked.

"Yes, thanks, but I was furious. I flogged my guts out last night trying to get it done when I wasn't in the mood, and then this morning I find out he's given Trish and Paul and half the others an extension 'till Monday."

"Well at least it won't be hanging over you all weekend," Rukhsana consoled. "I bet you're looking forward to seeing your Mum."

"Yeah, it seems like ages, sometimes I can't even picture her face properly," Yasmin confided, beginning to relax in the gentle eddies of conversation.

"I missed my Mum like crazy when I first came here, I'd never been away from home before, not even for a night. I couldn't cope with having a room all to myself, either, I was so scared and I missed my sisters talking, and fighting over drawers and hangers and all that. Now I couldn't manage without my own room, I don't know how I'll ever go back."

"You won't have to, will you?"

"I don't know," Rukhsana sighed. "They want me to, of course. It's like they did me this really big favour letting me come here 'cos a lot of our relatives told them they shouldn't and college was full of sex and drugs and bad people, so now I ought to do what they want, you know, make them happy by going home and getting married. If I don't everybody will say `I told you so' and my parents will be shamed in front of the whole community."

"Couldn't you get a job?"

"I suppose so, but some people would say I was getting like a gori and I must be going with white men. And my Mum's already worrying that soon I'll be too old to get a good husband. I can just hear all the arguments," she added wearily.

"Do your parents believe in `arranged marriages' then?" Yasmin asked surprised. She had thought Rukhsana's parents must be very liberal to have a daughter like Rukhsana.

"Don't give me that `arranged marriages' stuff,"

49

Rukhsana said sharply. "That's what white people go on about all the time. It's not a question of `arranged marriages', my parents wouldn't make me marry anyone I didn't want to. In fact, they're always asking if I've met any nice Muslim boys up here, they'd be ecstatic if I fell for someone myself, as long as he was a Muslim. The problem is I just want to get a job and get on with my own life, I don't want to marry anyone at all."

"Can't you tell them that?"

"Not really. I don't want to make them unhappy, they worry about getting us settled. I know it just wears them out."

"It sounds really complicated," Yasmin looked subdued.

"Anyway, what time are you going on Friday?" Rukhsana said briskly.

"Four-ish. I get there about half-past six."

"Will your Mum's boyfriend be there?"

"What, Rod? Oh, yes, he lives with us now."

"How do you get on with him?"

"Fine. He's a bit way-out, you know, a sort of aging hippy, I thought he was dead embarrassing at first and I used to tell Mum to keep him away when my friends came round. I didn't want them to see his hair 'cos he's got a ponytail, a little straggly one, and he wears weird clothes!"

"So what changed?"

"I suppose it was when we all went on holiday, he was a really good laugh and I stopped being ashamed of him 'cos we didn't know anyone. And I could see Mum really loved him, so in the end I gave up being such a pain!"

"Atiya asked me about your Mum and Dad the other day. I told her to ask you. Has she said anything?"

"No," Yasmin said surprised. "What did she want to know?"

"Well, she asked if they were divorced, so I said I didn't know. I never said they weren't married in the first place. I didn't know what you wanted people to know, it's none of their business, really."

"I don't mind people knowing my parents weren't

married. Why, do you think I should?" Yasmin asked as she saw Rukhsana's hesitant expression.

"People like Atiya can be more traditional than you think," Rukhsana said cautiously. "I mean she's got some very old-fashioned ideas, you'd be surprised. Of course, it's up to you, but I'd be careful who you tell your business to, there's a lot of gossip goes on and people notice you."

"What people?" Yasmin was taken aback at the idea that people noticed her without her realising. "Why should anyone notice me?"

"Yasmin, of course people notice you," Rukhsana laughed, "you've got dark skin, haven't you? I couldn't help noticing you, for a start, but also white people notice you 'cos you're different, they notice all of us."

"Well, sometimes people ask me if I'm Italian or Greek, or things like that," Yasmin conceded. "But that's only occasionally, and then I just put them right."

"How do you put them right?"

"I tell them I'm English and my Dad was from Pakistan, but I was born here. It's not a problem," Yasmin insisted defensively, but even as she said it she remembered a boy called John Griffiths who used to whisper ugly words behind her in geography lessons. She remembered the horror she felt when they started a topic on `India and Overpopulation' and John said loudly, `Come on, Yaz, you know all about this, why don't you tell us?' She never forgave that teacher for ignoring it and carrying on with the topic, she felt herself blushing hotly through half the lessons and was convinced everyone was looking at her. Another memory flashed through her mind of her and Jenny at a fair one August Bank Holiday and a crowd of older boys following them round the stalls, taunting her with, `Paki, go home!' She felt the hot shame and confusion returning as she thought about it, but she remembered laughing it off at the time, saying they were just ignorant. She could see herself in Jenny's kitchen afterwards, saying, `They made a mistake, they're so thick they can't even see who's Pakistani and who isn't.'

"Well, sometimes people did call me other things, you know, prejudiced things," Yasmin began to admit.

"Racist things," Rukhsana interrupted. "That's what it is, they were being racist."

"Well, whatever you call it, yes, it did happen. But they were just stupid people and I didn't care about them, I've got lots of friends, I don't need to worry about people like that. Anyway, what are you getting at?"

"Nothing," Rukhsana replied. "Nothing at all. I was just saying don't think people don't notice you and aren't dead nosy about who you are. And don't be surprised if Atiya starts asking daft questions. By the way, I was going to ask you, do you want to come to the Asian Society next week? We're having a little party for Diwali on Wednesday and I think you'd enjoy it."

"Can anyone go?" Yasmin asked doubtfully.

"Of course. Next week's a party for us and our friends, so there'll be lots of different people there. But you can come to any meeting you like, you don't have to join up properly straight away, you can just come and see what it's like."

"Thanks for inviting me, but I don't know anything about Diwali, I don't want to intrude on other people's celebrations."

"Don't be silly," Rukhsana laughed. "It's not my festival either, you know, it's a Hindu thing, we just celebrate everybody's special days, it's more fun that way. That's what they do in India."

"But I haven't got anything to wear," Yasmin protested lamely.

"You've got loads of nice party clothes, just wear what you feel like. Or you could wear something of mine," Rukhsana reassured her.

"Okay, I'll think about it," Yasmin agreed, "but I don't think I can come to the other meetings. I know you think it's okay, but I don't think anyone else would, really, would they?"

"Why not?" Rukhsana countered, "Asha's already asked me if you want to join."

"But I wouldn't know what anyone was talking about, I don't know anything about India or Pakistan."

"Asia's much bigger than India and Pakistan, there are lots of places I don't know anything about. The question is, do you want to know?"

"I don't know. There are lots of other things I'm just as interested in, like the French Film Society and my youth club. Why should I have to be interested just 'cos of my Dad who I've never seen hardly?" she finished rebelliously.

"Okay, okay!" Rukhsana put her hands up in mock defence. "Forget I mentioned it. Nobody says you have to be interested in anything."

"You just want me to join your club, that's why you're friends with me," Yasmin suggested sulkily.

"Is that what you think?" Rukhsana looked at her seriously, "Because if it is..."

"No, of course it isn't," Yasmin denied, poking the crumbs on her plate vehemently. "I'm fed up of talking about all this, let's talk about something nice."

"Such as?" Rukhsana smiled, raising an eyebrow.

"How are things with Vikram? Has he asked you out yet?" Yasmin asked teasingly.

"No, you must be joking!" Rukhsana laughed."But I think we may be getting there. We're supposed to be getting together on Monday to sort out the lights and fireworks and things for next Wednesday, so you never know..."

"Will you say something if he doesn't?" Yasmin asked.

"I couldn't, I'd be so embarrassed if he'd never thought anything like that, I'd just die!" Rukhsana replied, appalled at the thought.

"You sound just like someone at school!" Yasmin laughed affectionately. "Anyway, it's not very `right on' of you, women can ask men out these days, you know. The worst he can do is say no, and that's not so terrible, is it?"

"Yes it is," said Rukhsana passionately. "Believe me, I'd never live it down!"

"I'm going to get some more tea, do you want some?"

Yasmin was fishing in a rucksack pocket for her purse.

"No thanks, I'll burst if I have any more tea today, but can you get me one of those Danish pastry things and some orange juice, please? Here's a pound."

"Put it away, I'll get these," Yasmin said, getting up from her seat, and she made her way back to the counter, thinking how nice it was having lunch out for a change, rather than always snatching time in their rooms between other commitments. Rukhsana had been right about that. Yasmin felt so much better now they had resumed the easy sharing of their thoughts and feelings that had become her reference point over the past few dizzying weeks.

5

DIFFERENCES

The inter-city train gently disengaged its wheels and slid away from the platform, the smooth whine of its engine rising rapidly to a controlled scream as it accelerated past shunting yards and engine sheds. Yasmin folded her jacket and draped it over her small red rucksack and carrier bag of work files, placed squarely on the seat beside her to discourage prospective occupants. The carriage was warm and quiet, filled with commuters and weekend travellers. A trim man in a dark grey suit sat diagonally opposite Yasmin, his briefcase beside him and a sheaf of typed papers spread over the table, which he was skimming through, making notes in the margins with a freshly sharpened pencil.

Yasmin settled back in her seat and stared out of the window, watching factories and back yards of terraced houses stream past the window. She felt deliciously anonymous and undefined sitting in this railway carriage surrounded by people who knew nothing about her. If she wanted, she could just get off at any station along the way, book into a hotel and pretend to be someone completely different, no-one would know. She found train journeys very romantic and liberating. She imagined herself disengaging from her own specific cluttered life, just as the train disengaged from the platform buffers, skimming the tracks above her world, barely in contact with the surface.

The rows of semi-detached houses and neat back gardens slowly gave way to brown ploughed fields and green hills rising gently above winding rivers. It was modest, undramatic country, acres of rich farmland, tamed and precisely fenced, and huddled red-brick villages connected by miles of empty, twisting minor roads. Yasmin had always despised such landscapes, associating them with the small-minded parochialism of her mother's family, who lived in Midlands villages just like these. But now she saw a kind of beauty in the delicate wintry trees silhouetted against a leaden grey sky, and the tangled hedgerow lining a field of faded, trampled corn stubble. She could imagine feeling nostalgic for these scenes in years to come, linking them to her student days and this first crazy, exciting term.

She felt a little as if she had lived a whole lifetime at university already; Rukhsana, Sharon, Trish, Fiona, they all seemed more real and close at this moment than her mother or Jenny. They had shifted everything in her life and created a new landscape, especially Rukhsana. Yasmin wondered if things might not have been a lot easier if she had never met Rukhsana. She tried to imagine what would have happened if she had got a place in hall with the other first years, but the picture she formed seemed rather flat and limited without Rukhsana. She always felt a kind of reserve between her and Sharon, like an invisible, transparent barrier, though she could not say who had originally erected it, if either of them had. When something significant happened it was Rukhsana she rushed to tell, not Sharon.

But there were some things she couldn't even talk to Rukhsana about, like this Diwali party, and the Asian Society meetings. She just didn't feel right going and she didn't know how to explain that to Rukhsana, she felt she would be pretending to be something she wasn't. She was different from Rukhsana and Shahnaz and the rest of them, she felt sure of that, although she could also see that they were very different from any idea she had previously had of Asian women herself. The question was, did she feel more like them, or more like Jenny, who she had grown up with, or was she just different from everyone? And did it matter, anyway? Maybe Mum was right after all, maybe groups and labels don't matter. She leaned her head against the window, thinking about how her mother hated organisations and rules and doing things in groups. Then she turned to her bag of files and dug out a brown envelope of letters. She pulled out a letter from her mother received that day.

`My dear Yasmin,' it read, `I hope this letter catches you in time, it's just to say that we'll meet you at the station on Friday, so don't go rushing off to get a bus. We'll be outside the ticket barrier. My only daughter's never been away from home for so long and she's not traipsing about on the bus when we've got a car to fetch her in! I'm looking forward to seeing you so much and I've got so many questions to ask you!

`I'm glad you're making friends and enjoying yourself so much, but it's only what I expected, you have such a friendly, open nature. I know you don't like me saying this, but you must be careful not to let people take advantage of your good nature, you know what a tendency you have to go overboard about your friends. I'm particularly pleased you've made so many friends in your own year. Rukhsana sounds nice, but remember she's older than you and she'll be leaving soon, so you don't want to get too attached to her - I don't want you to get hurt, my love. It's more important to have good loyal friends in your own year, who can be with you throughout your time at college. Why don't you invite one of your friends up here for a weekend? What about Sharon, or Fiona? You know they'd be more than welcome.

`This was only meant to be a short note, so I'd better stop now. Rod sends his love. Look after yourself. Lots of love and kisses, Mum.'

Yasmin read through her other letters. One from her friend Lisa, who was doing teacher training in Liverpool, a card from Rod, and three letters from Jenny, who had started in a bank after her `A' levels and always said she never wanted to go to university. The dry, air-conditioned heat of the carriage made her feel drowsy and after Derby she fell into a doze, rocked by the swaying motion of the train, with her letters still in her lap.

Maggie Shaw shuddered involuntarily as an icy wind

blew down the platform, whipping showers of raindrops under the corrugated iron roof. She pulled her woollen scarf tighter round her neck and dug her hands deep into the pockets of her old anorak. All her life she had hated waiting and she was no better now. She paced slowly up and down an imaginary line, glancing up frequently at the television monitor suspended from a metal beam above them, which indicated that Yasmin's train was on time. She was tall and heavily built, with broad hips and shoulders, and a healthy glowing face, red-cheeked from the cold wind and from rushing across the bridge from the station entrance. Her hair was short and curly, a light auburn colour, streaked throughout with silvery grey, and she had striking grey-green eyes, with tiny creases appearing at the corners.

"Don't tell me you're nervous," Rod teased. He was leaning against a wall, smoking a cigarette and watching her.

"So what if I am?" Maggie retorted, stopping to look at him. "She's my only child and she's growing up too fast, it's frightening. I feel like I don't know what she's going to say or do next."

"I thought you didn't mind what she did as long as she's happy?"

"I know, but I do worry, she seems so intense about Rukhsana."

Rod shrugged his shoulders and dropped his cigarette end on the floor, grinding it in with his heel. "Don't worry. She can't do any worse than you did to your parents," he said flippantly.

"Thanks, you're a great help," Maggie muttered and walked away again.

It was dark and raining in Sheffield, but Yasmin still recognised the deep wooded cutting on one side of the tracks, and the long warehouses and factory sheds on the other, looming in the white glare of industrial arc lights. She stepped off the warm train into a biting wind and instantly spotted Rod's bright red cagoule and her Mother's round face and familiar tall figure. For a brief moment she felt almost shy and then she forgot her hesitation as she was caught up in a vigorous hug from her mother and loud greetings from Rod.

"You look tired, love, are you all right?" Maggie said, holding Yasmin away from her again and scrutinising her face.

"'Course I am, I just fell asleep on the train," Yasmin assured her and took her arm as they walked back towards the footbridge.

"It's all these late nights," Rod called out, following them. "Partying 'till daylight. I know what you students get up to!"

"You're just jealous!" Yasmin laughed. "Anyway I get my work done."

"Which is more than he ever did, so don't take any notice," Maggie interrupted. "Now, I hope you're hungry because there's loads of tea, I've cooked your favourite, lasagna, and apple pie for afters."

"Oh, great," Yasmin enthused, "I didn't get anything on the train 'cos I was hoping there'd be a nice tea."

They got into the car, a rusting old Datsun estate which they had bought when Rod moved in, and Maggie drove them home through driving rain and the glare of other cars' headlights. They climbed up from the city centre nestling in the valley to the outer suburbs perched on a crescent of windswept hills reaching westwards into the Pennines.

Maggie's house was in a small terrace high up on a hillside, with a narrow garden at the back, dropping away steeply, and a sweeping view of the valley beyond. She could probably afford more now, and Rod could definitely buy a bigger house with his youth work salary. But they stayed on here because Maggie loved the view and their elderly neighbour, Mrs Wilkinson, depended on her. Maggie was wary of change for the sake of it and knew what it was to have the rug pulled from under her feet. She hung on tight to the security of her cosy home and the happiness she had found there, it was worth more than extra bedrooms or a garage for the car.

The house was warm inside and smelt of cooking, Yasmin sat at the big kitchen table with Tibby their cat on her knee, chatting to her mother, while Maggie boiled some vegetables. Rod had gone out again straight away to do his Friday night youth work session and promised to bring back something from the off licence later.

"So, tell me what your days are like, I want to hear all about it," Maggie said, lighting the gas under a pan of carrots.

"Oh, you know more about it than me," Yasmin replied.

"Only bits of it, I see snatches of students' lives here and there, but I'm a secretary for the lecturers, not the students. Anyway, I want to hear about you, not anyone else."

"Well, most days I walk into the university after breakfast and go to lectures and classes... "

"What are your lecturers like ?"

"Oh, a mixture, some of them are real absent-minded professor types and others are quite young and trendy, they're mostly really nice and they've given me quite good marks so far." Yasmin stroked the cat as she looked around the kitchen at the familiar things, familiar, yet different because now she noticed them.

"So you're managing the work okay ?"

"Yeah, I can do it when I get down to it, it's more finding the time with everything else. Also, it always takes longer than I think it will and I end up in a right panic at the end."

"You were the same at school with your homework," Maggie smiled, fondly and then she said softly, "Your father was the same too."

Yasmin drew in her breath and looked up at her mother quickly to try and gauge her mood.

"Yasmin," she came over to the table and sat on the edge of a chair beside her daughter, her eyes were grey and serious. "I know I should have talked about him more before. I'm sorry. But he hurt me a lot and it took me so many years to forget him, I don't want to start remembering now." Maggie's voice shook a little with emotion as she spoke and Yasmin felt a slight panic, she didn't want to see her mother cry, she felt too shaky herself.

"It doesn't matter, Mum," she reassured, "I'm not that interested."

"Yes, it does matter," Maggie contradicted earnestly. "One day I won't be here any more and it's selfish of me to take all these memories to the grave with me, they belong to you too."

"Rubbish, you'll be around for years," Yasmin laughed nervously. "You don't have to start thinking about all that yet, Mum, you're still young."

"No-one knows what lies ahead. Just give me a bit of time, my love, and I'll tell you what I can. You never showed any interest before and that suited me fine, but if you want to know now, then you shall know, we'll have to do something about it," Maggie rose decisively and returned to the cooker. "Now I think these vegetables are done. Can you lay the table ?"

Yasmin nudged Tibby off her lap and leapt up, thankful for a postponement of this difficult conversation, and went over to the old carved sideboard where they kept the cutlery. Maggie turned on the radio for the News and `The Archers', which she listened to every evening in the week, except if Rod was away at the weekend on a youth service camp, when she waited 'till the Sunday morning omnibus, lying alone in bed with a cup of tea and Tibby curled up on the quilt beside her.

After dinner they retired to the newly decorated front room, which Yasmin admired strenuously, and sincerely. It did indeed look brighter and more sophisticated than the heavy browns and beiges they had lived with since her mother bought the house. Something in her still resisted the change though, feeling it was more Rod's doing than her mother's and that he had waited for her to go away to do it. She had to admit she liked the creamy peach-coloured walls and the charcoal grey carpet, she just wasn't sure it was `them', meaning herself and her mother.

They settled down in front of the gas fire with cups of coffee, Yasmin on the settee and Maggie in her big square leather armchair with a couple of cushions behind her.

"Your room's still the same," Maggie said seeming to read Yasmin's thoughts. "I'm afraid I haven't even hoovered it since you went. Tibby sleeps on your bed every afternoon, she loves it up there."

"It's the sunniest place in the house," Yasmin agreed, "I hope it's nice tomorrow I'm dying to go for a good long walk."

"What else would you like to do? I've got nothing planned. Are you going to see Jenny?"

"Definitely, I haven't rung her yet, I've been so disorganised. Maybe I could see her tomorrow afternoon, or on Sunday? She's the only person I want to see, otherwise I was looking forward to just flopping at home and not seeing anyone."

"You're not overdoing it at college, are you?"

"No, I'm fine," Yasmin insisted, feeling irritated by her mother's questions. She felt inexplicably out of sorts. She had wanted to feel relaxed and to slip easily back into the cosiness of home. But instead she felt uneasy and upset by the earlier conversation. She felt they were both trying just a little bit too hard to pretend everything was fine when it was obvious that something was different. She didn't want to have to explain things to her mother. She wanted her to know without explanation, by some kind of osmosis or instinct, like she always knew before, like she guessed when Brian ditched Yasmin in the fifth year, or when she and Jenny had been arguing.

She looked at her mother and her mind was full of questions, questions for Rukhsana and questions for Maggie, which she could not ask. Instead she just let the questions tumble through her mind as she stared into the quietly hissing gas fire. `What if they'd called me Ruth or Annie?' she thought, thinking of her cousins' names. `What if I'd had auburn hair and green eyes like Mum? What if my skin was lighter? What if my Dad had stayed? Would I have been brought up a Muslim? Would they have got married? Would I know how to cook aloo gobi? Would I know who Anil Kapoor is?'

"You're looking very thoughtful, dear, are you sure you're not worrying about anything?" Maggie asked gently. Her daughter seemed different, preoccupied. Maybe she was waiting for Maggie to say more about Farooq, but Maggie knew she could not tonight. It was painful even to think his name in her head, Farooq, a name she had barely spoken for fifteen years, not even to Rod, who had tried to make her talk about it. But she wasn't one of his teenage truants, to be subjected to his `non-directive counselling', and she didn't want him interfering with Yasmin's peace of mind either, no matter how many anti-racist courses he'd been on. Yasmin was her responsibility and she'd done fine up to now, she didn't need any advice about mixed race children and positive self-images. They didn't know when to let well alone some of these youth workers and Rod was no better than the rest of them, however much she loved him.

"Mum, I'm just tired. I've been up late every night this week. Can I have a bath in a bit?"

"Yes, of course, there's plenty of hot water. You can use the big pink towel, it's in the airing cupboard, you know, and your bubble bath's still there that Mrs Wilkinson got you last Christmas."

"How is she ?"

"Oh, doing very well, you'll have to pop round and see her, I told her you were coming home, she got quite excited. Her hip's been much better since her son had the central heating put in. But she worries like mad about the bills, even though half the radiators are turned off."

"Did he come to stay, then, her son?"

"Did he heck! He asked Rod to find a plumber to do the job and he sent a cheque when it was done. She moved in here while they did the work," Maggie sniffed in disgust. "You will go and see her, won't you love, she's always saying you're like a grand-daughter to her, and she's done a lot more for you than your own relations ever did, looking after you after school every day all those years."

"Of course I'll go and see her," Yasmin assured her, thinking crossly that her mother was more concerned about Mrs Wilkinson and Jenny than she was about Yasmin. `Why doesn't she know the right questions to ask?' Yasmin thought. But she knew that really it was up to her to raise the things she wanted to and she also knew that she couldn't. She could think about it all the way home on the train and she could write about it in her diary, but she could not talk to her mother about it.

"I think I'll have that bath now," she said suddenly. "Is that okay?"

"Whatever you want, love," Maggie smiled, "you look like you could do with a good long soak to relax you, go on."

Yasmin collected her rucksack and bags from the kitchen and took them upstairs to the attic, which had been her room since she was old enough not to fall down the stairs. The wooden-framed dormer window faced the back of the house and had no curtains. From it you could see out across the valley to the high-rise flats on the other side, and westwards towards open moorland and the hills beyond. Yasmin unfastened the catch on the large single window and it tilted open at the bottom. A roaring blast of wind rushed into the room and she leaned forward against the high sill, drinking in the cold, fresh air and the great dark spaces beyond. Heavy rain spattered against the window, which shook in the wind howling round the rooftops. Yasmin stood there for a while looking out over a panorama of twinkling orange street lights cloaking the valley sides and floor. Out to the west there was a dark void, where she knew great lonely hills loomed. In her mind's eye she could see swollen streams tumbling down the hillsides and the storm tearing at stunted thorn trees and tall, swaying pines. She loved the timeless hostility of the hills at night, she liked to imagine them emptied of the day's walkers and trippers and restored to their primeval state. She shivered as her skin prickled with goose bumps and quickly banged the window shut. The room fell silent again, apart from the faint sound of the television drifting up the stairs from the front room.

Yasmin felt better alone in her own room, this was the sanctuary she had been looking forward to and she pottered around for a while, unpacking her few clothes and setting out her books and files on the old table in the corner where she always used to do her homework. She laid her hairbrush and slides out on the pine dressing table, which she and her mother had assembled from a kit on her twelfth birthday, to the accompaniment of helpless giggles. As she turned away, she caught sight of her face in the mirror, serious and drawn. She stopped and sat down on the stool in front of the wide mirror, looking hard and searchingly at the face she knew so well, but she could not detach herself enough to imagine what other people saw. Opening a drawer, she rummaged until she found a long silk scarf, patterned in turquoise and green. She wrapped it lightly around her head and shoulders and tried to imagine it was the end of a sari, or a dupatta like Rukhsana sometimes wore with her suits. Concentrating very hard, she began to see that perhaps, in the eyes of people who had never seen her before, it would not look incongruous, but completely natural. She supposed her hair was very dark brown, almost black, and her skin was certainly more brown than any other colour, in fact, she was probably darker than Atiya, who was very fair, but she still didn't feel like Atiya. She felt like Yasmin Shaw, daughter of Maggie Shaw, an ordinary Sheffield girl who was good at French, had a cat called Tibby and liked hill-walking. Sighing, she put the scarf back in the drawer and hurried down the attic stairs to run her bath.

6

PAINFUL QUESTIONS

The next day was fresh and rain-washed, water dripped from the gutters and the sun slowly dried long shining puddles lying in dips in the pavement. Ragged clouds raced across a cold blue sky and when Yasmin looked out of her window she could see clearly the dark purple-brown moors lining the horizon. She woke up in an optimistic, sociable mood and chatted cheerfully through breakfast, seeming to have forgotten her brooding silences of the night before. Maggie was relieved and felt she had been over-anxious. She and Yasmin spent a happy hour over at Mrs. Wilkinson's after breakfast and Maggie soon felt as if Yasmin had never been away. She noticed that Yasmin found all sorts of entertaining little details to tell Mrs Wilkinson about her life at university that she had never mentioned to her mother. But at the moment Maggie was too worried about the things she had not told Yasmin herself to care about what happened in the laundry room in hall or what the French student was like who ran Yasmin's conversation class.

Yasmin had arranged to meet Jenny for lunch in town, after she had finished work. `I wouldn't have worked on a Saturday if I'd known you were coming. Why didn't you tell me earlier?' Jenny had said on the phone the night before, and had teased Yasmin about forgetting old friends in her wild social life at college. She finished at twelve-thirty and Yasmin was to meet her by the fountain near the town hall. Yasmin sat on a wooden bench beside the stagnant pool, strewn with litter. She watched the Saturday morning shoppers hurrying by in their winter coats, shoulders hunched and collars turned up against the wind, an endless flow of greys and browns and shades of blue, with an occasional splash of deep crimson or shell-suit pinks and greens. She scoured the faces streaming by, looking for Jenny's small, determined figure and laughing face. She remembered their countless meetings by this fountain, before Saturday morning shopping sprees, or nights out in town. She remembered wandering back past here, arms linked, after an evening of crazy hilarity, daring each other to totter round the rim of the fountain without falling in, before racing to catch the last bus home. When Jenny did appear in the crowd, it took Yasmin a moment to recognise her.

"Hiya Yaz, sorry I'm late. Hope you're not frozen!" she panted.

Her face was flushed from walking fast and Yasmin noticed she was quite heavily made up, with pale blue eye shadow deepening to mauve and bright red lipstick accentuating her small mouth. Her blonde hair had been permed into tight curls and was pinned back by a large red clip on the back of her head, from which a few curls were escaping to dangle down by her cheeks. She was wearing a dark blue belted coat and black court shoes with tapering heels and she looked very old and stylish to Yasmin, much older than the schoolgirl in faded jeans Yasmin remembered walking to the dams with on Sunday afternoons, or reading magazines with in her bedroom, laughing at the beauty tips and sighing over the love stories.

"Hi, you look so posh and you've had your hair done different. You make me look like a right impoverished student!" Yasmin laughed, looking down ruefully at her old grey jacket and black leggings.

"Well, you are," Jenny retorted. "Anyway, we have to dress like this, it's expected, you should see some of them! `Oh, my dear, I couldn't touch the copier, I might break a nail!'" She mimicked an imaginary bank clerk and pirouetted for Yasmin's benefit. They both giggled and then, as if with the same thought, set off for their usual department store coffee shop, Jenny tucking her hand under Yasmin's arm as they strode along.

They sat opposite each other at a small table in the coffee shop, on which there was barely room for their assemblage of plates, cups, miniature milk jugs and stainless steel tea and coffee pots.

"So, how's it going?" Jenny asked, when they had settled themselves and transferred the remains of the last hurried snack to an empty table nearby. "You sounded like you were having a whale of a time in your letter, I'm really jealous."

"It's great," Yasmin replied enthusiastically. "... And thanks for all your letters, it was really nice getting them, I was a bit lonely right at the beginning, you know, a bit homesick. But I got over it really fast and now I'm so at home there I felt a bit odd coming back here last night, like I was just a visitor or something. I'm sure Mum thought I was really off with her."

"Were you?"

"No, I was just tired and sometimes I wish Rod still had his own flat. I didn't mind when I was at home all the time too, but yesterday I just felt like it was their house and I was a visitor. Mum was even telling me where to find the towels, as if I didn't know!"

"I'm sure she didn't mean it like that," Jenny contradicted. "She was probably just fussing because she was so excited to have you home."

Yasmin knew she was right, but she felt if they continued on this subject she would end up in a bad mood with Jenny as well.

"How are you, anyway?" she asked.

"Oh, not so bad. The job's awful. They bitch about each other like anything and the office is like a morgue, you can't say a word out of place with people breathing down your neck all the time. It's worse than school! But I see Jill and Pete and people at the weekend and we have a good time, nothing like your parties and discos, I suppose, but I enjoy myself."

"How's your Mum?"

"She's not too good, they're going to have to take her in again soon for some more chemotherapy and she's really dreading it. She's been talking to this herbalist, or homeopath or something, about not having it done, but

Dad thinks she should trust the hospital. He doesn't believe in private medicine, and he thinks Pat, that's the herbalist, just wants to make money out of us."

"What do you think?" Yasmin asked, concerned and a little unnerved at the thought of Jenny's mother having cancer.

"Oh, I don't know," Jenny replied wearily. "There doesn't seem to be anyone you can ask and they're always so busy at the hospital. Pat seems nice enough, but how do we know she knows what she's talking about? I suppose it's up to Mum, though sometimes she can't even think straight, she feels so ill."

"It must be really hard for all of you," Yasmin said, feeling inadequate and wishing she could say something really useful.

"Oh, we get by," Jenny smiled. "It's not all doom and gloom, you know! Mum always has a laugh about things, she's really funny sometimes, she cheers me up."

"Do people at work know?"

"Not really. Most of them I don't bother with, but there's this woman called Grace, she's a bit older and she's got kids, and I told her about Mum. She's really nice, but we don't see each other out of work because she's busy with her family, I don't know if she's told anyone else. It's much harder making friends than it was in school, I thought it'd be easier."

"It's dead easy at university, everyone's really friendly," Yasmin admitted.

"I know, you jammy so-and-so, you keep telling me!" Jenny teased with an edge of resentment. "But how do you go on for money, with all this drinking and dancing and eating out?"

"Terrible! I'm nearly broke already, I don't know how I'm going to last 'till Christmas...and I don't even drink that much."

"Oh yes? And the rest!" Jenny scoffed. "So, who are all these friends you're always going out with? You said about Sharon in your letter, and the Indian girl..."

"Rukhsana, she's Pakistani."

"Yeah, her. Anyone else?"

"No-one important. There's Trish who's on my course, I see her all the time but I don't like her that much, and Sharon's got a nice friend called Fiona that we often meet up with. I like some of Rukhsana's friends, but I don't know them very well."

"Any blokes you fancy?"

"No, not at all," Yasmin laughed. "We're all good mates and we go out in a big crowd, men and women. It's nice just being friends with boys without having to worry about whether they fancy you or not. Anyway, tell me who you've seen recently."

They talked about old school friends for a while and Jenny filled Yasmin in on all the news of friends who had stayed in Sheffield, and things she had heard about friends away at college. There was plenty to talk about, but the conversation seemed shallow and unsatisfying to Yasmin, she wanted to break through to some other deeper level, but she didn't know how to do it. She began to feel frustrated as she noticed they had already been there nearly an hour.

"It's funny meeting Rukhsana," she said when a pause occurred in the conversation. "She makes me think about my Dad and what he was like, you know, with her being from Pakistan too. I keep wanting to find out more. Mum says she'll tell me, but I feel mean for asking her 'cos it upsets her to talk about him."

"I thought you hated him?" Jenny challenged. "Your friend, whatever her name is, surely she doesn't think he did the right thing leaving you like that?"

"No, of course she doesn't. I still think he must be an awful person to have just left us, and selfish and all that. But it's not just him I'm thinking about, it's me as well."

"What do you mean? What about you?" Jenny looked puzzled and frustrated.

"Well, I'm not just English like my Mum, am I? A bit of me's Pakistani too and I don't know anything about it."

"But why should you? You never lived over there, your life is here. Anyway, it never bothered you before, and it

70

shouldn't bother anyone who cares about you. It certainly doesn't bother me," Jenny announced defiantly.

"I never said it did," Yasmin's eyes widened in surprise, surely Jenny didn't think she was getting at her? "I just meant I want to know more about where I've come from, it's no big deal."

"I thought you came from Sheffield," Jenny responded sulkily.

"You know what I mean."

"No, I don't, I think it's rubbish all this about where you've come from, I haven't the foggiest where my family come from. Does it matter? I suppose this friend's been telling you all about Pakistan, then?"

"Not really, I mean, we're just friends, she's not exactly giving me lectures on it, is she? I just pick up odd things from listening to her talk."

"That's nice," said Jenny sarcastically. Yasmin fell silent, her mind struggling with the last few exchanges, wondering why Jenny appeared to feel so threatened. She began to fold an empty sugar packet into a small triangle. It was easier when they had things to do, she thought, when they were at school they were always doing something; going shopping for magazines and stationery and cheap jewellery; taking picnics out with Jenny's family dog in tow; doing their homework; writing letters to their French penfriends; the list was endless. Now it seemed such hard work, just meeting for a chat, it felt like they had to re-learn how to be friends.

"How's everyone at Ash Lodge?" Yasmin asked looking up to catch Jenny watching her thoughtfully.

"Fine," Jenny replied. "Jason and Linda and that lot are all wild about their new school, you know, going to `big' school now, they're full of it. I haven't been as much since you went away, though. I'm so tired when I get home from work and it's not the same traipsing across town on my own. Are you coming to the Christmas party? It should be after the end of your term."

"Wouldn't miss it," Yasmin replied brightly. "I told you I've started going to a youth club like it near the university, didn't I?"

"Yeah, you said in your letter, do any of your friends go?"

"No, but the other helpers are great, and sometimes we all go for a drink afterwards. Some of them are students, but there are all different people," Yasmin explained thinking of the three other students she had met at the club, two second years called Maureen and Hilary, and Ben, who was another first year and was really good at organising games and making the children laugh. She liked Ben, he was friendly and easygoing, sometimes they all went for a quick drink afterwards in the students' union and she and Ben could compare notes on their first term.

"So, what shall we do tonight?" Jenny asked, her mood lightening. "I'm meeting Jill and Pete and some others in the Sportsman at half-seven, but we don't have to stay with them."

"Actually, I was going to stay in with Mum," Yasmin replied apologetically. "Rod's going out so we've got the place to ourselves and I'm going back tomorrow so I'll feel really bad if I don't spend some time with her tonight."

"Oh, Yaz!" Jenny wailed reproachfully. "You've hardly said hello and now I'm not going to see you again for weeks."

"I know, but why don't you come down and stay with me for a weekend? You'd love it," Yasmin urged.

"And see what I'm missing? No thanks!" Jenny replied gloomily. "Anyway, I can't go away at the moment."

"Well, I'll be at home for four weeks at Christmas, we can all get together then and go out like old times," Yasmin suggested.

"Yes, I suppose Lisa will be back as well, we could get quite a crowd together. I'd really like to see everybody, wouldn't you?" Jenny replied, rallying at the thought of a big reunion. She looked at her watch and, alarmed at the time, said anxiously, "I'm afraid I'm going to have to go. I promised Dad I'd be back for three o'clock. Would you like to come home for a cup of tea?"

"No, sorry, I can't. Mum and I are going for a walk this afternoon and if we don't get moving it'll be dark before we get out."

They made their way out of the shop and parted a little awkwardly by Jenny's bus stop.

"Keep writing, won't you?" Jenny urged her. "I miss you, you know."

"I miss you too," Yasmin replied warmly. "Hope your Mum gets a bit better soon. I'll be home for ages at Christmas, so we can meet up as much as we want. Look, there's your bus! 'Bye, see you soon."

"Bye, Yaz."

They hugged each other quickly and shyly and then Yasmin began to walk away as Jenny moved down the bus queue. Waiting at her own bus stop, Yasmin wondered sadly if she and Jenny would be able to survive all these changes and still be friends. Coming home for the weekend had not been quite as she expected, she had looked forward to being made a fuss of, heralded as the adventurer returned. But instead she found people immersed in their own lives and herself irritable because she could not convey to them the quality of her new life and her new concerns.

Maggie parked the car in a muddy lay-by just off the main road, from which a footpath struck out over a stile and across open moorland towards the long craggy edge a couple of miles away. On one side, stretching to the horizon, lay endless dark reaches of peat bog and stubborn, wind-tugged heather, its August-blooming flowers shrivelled and brown on gnarled twigs. On the other side a gentle hillside of crackling, russet-coloured bracken sloped away into the valley, and beyond rose the interlocking curves and peaks of further hills. Yasmin knew all their names and had climbed them all, with her Mum and Jenny, or with the church youth club Jenny went to which Yasmin had attended intermittently. She felt a rush of affection for their familiar rounded shapes, as she got out of the car and quickly zipped up her cagoule. Maggie locked the car doors and they set off, over the stile and on to the ancient path trodden into spongy black peat from centuries of human passage across the moors. The wind was behind them, promising a tough walk back to the car, and occasionally the sun broke through the banks of grey cloud that had built up since the morning, a thin shaft of golden light skimming the hillsides trailing a pool of liquid gold and green and soft coppery brown.

They walked briskly, talking loudly so that the wind would not snatch their words away and watching the path ahead as it dipped and climbed and wound around boulders and squelchy peat bogs.

"How was Jenny?" Maggie called out over the whistle of the wind.

"She's a bit fed up with the job. We haven't got that much to talk about at the moment... in common, I mean, and I don't want to go on about what a good time I'm having."

"You don't have to go on about it, but I'm sure it does her good to hear your news, she's your friend, she likes to know what you're doing."

"Well, we didn't have enough time really. It'll be better at Christmas."

"I wouldn't let it slide, love, Jenny's a good friend. I drifted apart from a lot of my friends when I first left home, I know what it's like. You just get busy in your new life and you don't know what to talk about any more. And after I met your father I just stopped going home because I didn't want to lie to my Mum and Dad and I didn't have anything else to talk about."

"Didn't they know about him, then?"

"Not at first. I knew they'd hit the roof and I didn't know how long it was going to last. We lived in a secret world of our own, really. We hardly knew anyone apart from a couple of his student friends, and I lost touch with all my friends, I was completely taken up with him, head over heels." She fell silent, thinking back to those early days.

"So how did they find out?" Yasmin prompted.

"I told them when I got pregnant with you. I wrote to them, I didn't dare go home...and my father wrote back and said he disowned me and never wanted to see me again, I never heard anything from my Mum, one way or the other, I suppose she just didn't know what to do and I was so far away it seemed to them like I didn't care what they thought anyway."

"Why didn't you get married ?"

"I don't know, we told a lot of people we were married, like the landlord, so we could get a flat. But Farooq said he wanted to do it properly, take me back to Pakistan and have a big family wedding. Then I got pregnant and it seemed too late for all that and we didn't have the money to travel. We were happy as we were. I wasn't bothered about being married and we knew other student couples living together just like us, it seemed okay, very modern and liberated, I was quite proud of us. It was getting really fashionable then, you know, I thought by now nobody would be married, but things seem to have gone back, not forward, since then, young people are a lot more conventional now than we were."

"I'm not," Yasmin interrupted indignantly.

"I know you're not, my love," Maggie laughed putting her arm round Yasmin's shoulders affectionately. "But you're my daughter, aren't you?"

They paused by an outcrop of scattered grey boulders and found a large flat one to sit on for a while, its surface was cold and pitted, but it was sheltered from the wind and commanded a fine view across the moors.

"So why did my Dad leave in the end?" Yasmin asked.

"His father died suddenly and he had to go home to help his older brother sort out the family property and everything. That's what he told me, anyway. Well, the bit about his Dad was true, I was there when he got the telegram, he was devastated. I don't suppose he ever got over not having been there to say good-bye, things like that go very deep. Maybe he thought his father's death was his fault, he had some funny ideas about fate and retribution, however rational and scientific he pretended to be. I've gone round and round in circles over the years, wondering what was going on in his head those last few days. I tried talking to him, but he just kept telling me it was going to be all right and he'd be back as soon as he'd sorted everything out. I think he believed it at the time because he wanted to, but I knew better, I had such a bad feeling about him going, I just knew," Maggie shook her head and clenched her hands together, fingers interlocked.

"Oh, Mum, I'm sorry," Yasmin whispered and they hugged clumsily.

"It's all right, really," Maggie reassured letting go of Yasmin. "I hated him for it, but I don't think he meant to leave us, I think he really thought he'd be coming back."

"So why didn't he?" Yasmin pressed, she felt she had to know everything, they had come so far in the conversation. Maggie sighed and turned to look at Yasmin sadly.

"I don't know why I didn't tell you this before," she said slowly thinking hard. "Maybe it hurt too much to think about it. You see, he married someone else...one of his cousins. I didn't find out for nearly a year, I was out of my mind with worry about him. I got one phone call from the airport and he wrote me a letter when his flight arrived in Karachi...and that was it." She paused thoughtfully. "I wrote loads of letters to the address he'd given me," she continued. "But I don't know if he ever got them. I was so lonely, all on my own in London with no job and no money and you to look after, but I daren't leave the flat because I knew if he came back, that's where he'd go. I got myself a typewriter and did some work at home, and I did cleaning jobs. I used to leave you with this student I met through your Dad, Kavita, her name was, bless her, she was so good to me. They were Sri Lankan. I think about her when I hear about all these refugees, you know, her husband was a communist, they were both real militants. I hope they're all right." She seemed lost in thought.

"Who told you what happened in the end?" Yasmin asked.

"You remember I told you about your Dad's friend, Asad?"

"What, Mr Munir?"

"Yes. Well, he came to see me. He said he'd had a letter from his mother and she'd written all about your Dad's wedding. He said he'd come to see me straight away, I suppose it was good of him really, he needn't have bothered, but I was never sure how much to believe... He said the whole family made your father feel really bad for having stayed away when they needed him. Apparently they wanted him to get married straight away and there was no question of leaving again, the family business was in such a mess and they needed him there. That's what Asad said anyway. He seemed sincere, but he could have just been helping his mate out by giving me lots of excuses. I suppose I can imagine Farooq just caving in under the pressure and his own guilt, he was never very good at arguments."

"No wonder you hated him," Yasmin said angrily. "He could at least have written and told you what was going on. He couldn't have loved his cousin. Why didn't he say no?"

"I don't know, Yasmin, maybe he didn't want to say no, we'll never know what really happened. It's easier in lots of ways to think he's just a selfish bastard. It was certainly easier for me at the beginning. All those months I'd waited when he was already married to another woman, I was so angry, you can't imagine. After I found out, I just had to get out of London, get away from the memories. I was too proud to go back home so I came up here, I thought Yorkshire sounded far enough north to blow away the London cobwebs! No other reason. I'm glad I came, though, I've been happy here," she paused looking out across the moors, and then said, briskly, "Shall we walk on?"

They got up and carried on along the path as it climbed up the back of a small stony escarpment. As they continued, the ridge developed into high crags looking out over rolling bracken-covered hills.

"So what else do you want to know?" Maggie asked after they had walked in silence for a while.

"Oh, I don't know, ordinary things, really," Yasmin replied. "Like did he ever teach you any of his language? What food did he like? What did he like to do? Am I like him? You know, things like that."

"That's a lot of questions, and a lot of detail," Maggie laughed. "I think we'll have to do it in batches."

"I'm sorry, are you fed up of talking about him now ?" Yasmin asked anxiously.

"No, it's all right," Maggie replied. "I just hope I can answer all your questions. I didn't ask about half these things myself, you know, I wasn't that interested, in fact, I never thought to ask and he didn't give much away, he was quite a secretive person. We didn't used to talk like I can talk to Rod, but we understood each other all the same. We always talked in English of course...he lived a very English life really, I suppose he was trying to fit in."

"Did he tell you about Pakistan?"

"Not really, except when he used to talk about his childhood, he loved talking about the farm they lived on when he was a child."

"Was he a Muslim?"

"He was born a Muslim, but he wasn't very religious. I don't remember him praying at all, but he wouldn't eat pork, or meat that hadn't been slaughtered properly, so we never ate meat at all."

"Is that how you became a vegetarian?" Yasmin interrupted.

"Yes...though I might have been anyway, I never liked meat much and I hated cooking it. Your father knew where to get his meat, meat that had been killed the right way, but it was too far to go and too expensive on the tube from where we lived, so we became vegetarians. Kavita taught me some recipes and Farooq got used to vegetable stews and egg and chips. The only time he bothered to go and get some proper meat was during Ramadan, you know, his month of fasting. He used to keep some of the fasts, not every day, but he kept quite a few. I couldn't believe it at first, I used to tease him about it because usually he was so scathing about religion, he said it caused most of the wars in the world and we'd be better off without it. But I think he believed in it quite a lot, especially when his father died."

"Yesterday you said he used to leave things 'till the last minute, like me."

"Oh yes," Maggie laughed. "He left everything to the last minute, he was infuriating, he would never look ahead. I suppose, looking back on it, he just lived with his head in the sand when he was with me. He must have known it couldn't last the way he'd set it up, but he never told me, I thought we'd carry on for ever. The worst thing is not knowing what he really thought, that's why I put him out of my mind, it's too distracting. I could spend my whole life wondering if he still loved me when he married that other woman, wondering what he thinks of me now. It's not worth it," she turned to Yasmin. "That's why I don't want you to start fretting over it now, it's a dead end, Yasmin. I know there are things you want to know, you've got a right to know, but don't waste too much energy on it, your life's ahead of you, it's no use looking back, believe me." She spoke urgently and fervently but Yasmin was not sure she accepted the advice, though she understood it.

At four o'clock they turned back, as they realised the sky was turning pink over the far hills and nearer hillsides already lay in deep shadow. On the way back Maggie told Yasmin more about her father, how polite and kind he had been, how he had courted her in a respectful, old-fashioned manner that had contrasted sharply with other men she had met in London, how he had walked her home from the college every day and travelled miles from his digs across London every Sunday to take her out for afternoon tea. He did not appear to have been a very practical man, Maggie had sorted out all the details when they moved into an unfurnished flat together, but he liked to think of himself as head of the household and responsible for all of them. Maggie said he grew up fast when Yasmin was born and he realised the enormity of his responsibilities. When he got his degree, he could not get the sort of job he wanted, though he went for dozens of interviews and was over qualified for most of them, so he took a job on the Underground, often working nights and weekends to keep the three of them going.

"He doted on you," Maggie told her. "He loved to play with you, we both did. He was a good father for the short time he knew you, I have to give him that, even though he ended up leaving you. Do you remember any of that?"

"Not really," Yasmin replied, realising she had no happy memory of her father at all.

"Well, it's not surprising, he worked such long hours he didn't see you very much, and you were still very young when he left."

"Do I remind you of him?"

Maggie thought about this for a while.

"It's hard to say," she replied. "You're just yourself, you don't remind me of anybody, but sometimes you make me think about him, things you say or do, like yesterday when you said about your essays. You've got his colouring, of course, and his big brown eyes, but when I look at you I see Yasmin, I don't see Farooq. I suppose you're like him the way you think about things a long time before you say them, Mrs Wilkinson always says you're `right deep'!" Maggie mimicked her voice and they both laughed.

"Isn't it beautiful?" Yasmin paused to look at the stormy red sky above the dark outline of the hills.

"Lovely," Maggie breathed "It's been a wonderful autumn here, we've had so many good sunsets out the back at home, you'd have loved it."

"I'm dead jealous," Yasmin complained. "I do miss my attic window, my room in hall faces north, I think, so I never get to see the sunset."

"A small price to pay for the excitement of being at university, I think. Come on, race you to the stile!"

They ran the last few yards to the stile and jostled each other over, panting and laughing.

7

THE DIWALI PARTY

It was dark when Yasmin got back to her room on Sunday night. Rukhsana was out, so she unpacked her rucksack and settled down at her desk to make some more notes on the volume of Baudelaire they were studying. She had taken it home with her in the vain hope of being able to do some work in a spare moment, but there had been no spare moments at home and her mind was too full of other things on the train journeys. She could see very little chance now of writing an essay on Baudelaire's most famous work by Tuesday morning, having scarcely read a word of his poetry before in her life. Not only that, but there was also a linguistics essay to be done by Friday.

She sat with the book open on the table before her, staring at the words without seeing them. She read the same line several times without taking it in, `O douleur! o douleur! Le Temps mange la vie,...' Instead she found herself thinking back over the weekend and wondering about the Diwali party on Wednesday. In a way she was relieved that Rukhsana was not back, even though she wanted to see her, because she was no nearer a decision on the party. She had thought that maybe if she talked to her mother about her father everything else would become clearer, but knowing more about him did not seem to tell her anything about what she should do here and now, she still felt herself to be floating in a void with few signposts to follow.

She reached round to the side of the desk and switched her kettle on, maybe a drink would help concentrate her mind and fill the blank pages in her foolscap pad. She knew she was scared of writing this essay, which made it even harder to start. She was not sure what she was meant to be writing or how to get started, she had written about poems before, but never a whole work in one essay, it seemed absurdly ambitious to attempt in three days.

She began reading again and had reached the end of a poem described by the introduction as `embodying the essence of Baudelaire', when there was a brisk knock and, without waiting for a reply, Rukhsana swung open the door and poked her head round, leaning on the door handle.

"Hi! You're back!"

"Yes, come in," Yasmin smiled, pleased to see her lively face. "I've just put the kettle on, you must be psychic."

"Just fated to be in the right place at the right time!" Rukhsana laughed brightly, jumping on to the bed.

"You're very pleased with yourself. Has something happened?" Yasmin probed curiously.

"Swear you won't tell anyone?"

"Of course not! Who would I tell?"

"All right. I bumped into Vikram tonight when I went to the cashpoint in the union and, wait for it, he asked me if I wanted to go for a meal after we've done the lights and stuff tomorrow!"

"That's brilliant!" Yasmin exclaimed. "You see, he does like you. I bet he asks you out officially."

"I don't know, maybe he's just being friendly," Rukhsana said doubtfully.

"What? Ask you out for a meal when there's just the two of you?"

"But would he have asked me if we hadn't bumped into each other?"

"Of course he would, it's probably been on his mind for days," Yasmin said definitely, getting up to make the tea.

"Anyway, how was your weekend?"

"Okay. Well, it was a bit of a mixture, really. It felt weird being back there right in the middle of term."

"How was your Mum?"

"Oh, she's fine. We had some good talks, especially yesterday, she told me loads about my Dad and her. I was thinking about it all on the train. You know, I always thought of her as really ordinary, an ordinary Mum who looks after the house and cooks and goes out to work as a secretary and all that. But she's had an amazing life. Like she left home and went to London when she was seventeen, and then she met my Dad and her parents disowned her, and then she managed to survive after he left. I never thought of her as being a rebel like that, being so brave and doing so many things when she was just my age. And all I've ever done is go to school."

"I know what you mean," Rukhsana agreed. "My parents took a big risk selling up and moving here, and it was really hard for them at first, not speaking much English and facing the kind of racist abuse they got. I hardly ever think about it, but they weren't that much older than me."

"I always thought my Mum had a really quiet life, just like she does now, it's hard to imagine what she was like then." Yasmin continued thoughtfully, and she handed Rukhsana a mug of tea.

"Thanks. How was her bloke?" Rukhsana asked, blowing her tea gently to cool it.

"A bit of a pain, actually. He was just around too much when I wanted to talk to Mum. Like last night, he was supposed to be going out, but his friend cancelled because their little girl was ill or something, so he stayed in with us and we watched telly and played Scrabble. It was all right, but not what I wanted. And they've decorated the front room without asking me. I know that's his doing."

"Well, I suppose he does live there too," Rukhsana suggested.

"I know and he's nice. It's just he can be a bit bouncy and sometimes I don't feel like talking to him, I'm not a kid in his youth club."

"Sounds like he really wound you up."

"I think I wound me up! I was even in a funny mood with Jenny."

"Your best friend from school?"

"Yeah, she seemed really different. She was dressed all posh for her job in the bank and she made me feel like I was still at school. We used to be really close, like sisters, but we didn't feel that close yesterday, at least, I didn't."

"Have you been friends a long time then?"

"Since we started at secondary school. We came from different junior schools and we hated each other at first. We were in the same class, but I used to avoid her, I thought she was really loud and bossy. But then this gang of third year girls started picking on my friend Lisa when she was going home from school and Jenny scared them off for her. After that we got to know her a bit and she started sitting next to me in some lessons and I helped her with her French homework and other stuff. In the end we were best friends and we used to go out every weekend on walks and shopping and all sorts. It was sort of an accident that we first got to know each other, but we ended up getting on really well."

"That's like real sisters," Rukhsana pointed out. "You don't choose them, you're just born into the same house, but usually you manage to get along pretty well. My sisters are great. Sometimes it's good to be thrown together with people so you're forced to get along, I think it makes you a better person."

"I don't know about that," Yasmin frowned dubiously. "They have to be nice people to begin with, they don't just turn nice because you're putting up with them."

"I suppose so," Rukhsana assented. She paused and then said, "You'd get on really well with my sisters. How'd you like to come home with me next time I go?"

"I'd love to! Are you sure?" Yasmin asked, flattered. "Wouldn't your Mum mind?"

"Oh no!" Rukhsana laughed. "She loves having visitors! Only thing is, you'll have to be careful not to say anything about Vikram."

"Of course not."

"Good. That's that settled. I was thinking of going in a couple of weeks, if that's okay with you? Then I can stay up longer after term's finished and get some work done here."

"Doesn't it get really lonely in the holidays?" Yasmin asked.

"It does in here, it's like a morgue," Rukhsana admitted.

"The worst bit is the first weekend when everyone disappears, you see them all go off with their rucksacks and suitcases and you're left behind and it seems so quiet. But people who live out will still be around, like Atiya and Shahnaz, they pay rent all year so they might as well be living there."

"Is Vikram staying on then?"

"He might be," Rukhsana replied coyly. "But he's got nothing to do with it. I shall be working."

"Oh, of course!" Yasmin laughed.

"Anyway, I'm stopping you working now, aren't I?"

"It doesn't matter, I haven't a clue what I'm doing anyway," Yasmin assured her. "In fact I might have to get help if I don't get anywhere with it tonight."

"Have you thought any more about Wednesday?" Rukhsana asked casually.

"I'd like to come, if that's all right with you," Yasmin replied, equally casually.

"Of course it is. Don't go into dinner, then, there'll be loads to eat at the party."

"Will you be going from here?"

"Yes. Don't worry, I won't leave without you!"

"It's just that I don't know where to go," Yasmin explained hurriedly.

"And it's no fun going to a party on your own when you hardly know anyone," Rukhsana finished off for her. "Anyway, I need you to give me moral support for when I see Vikram. Imagine if tomorrow's a flop, I'll feel awful on Wednesday."

"Tomorrow won't be a flop," Yasmin insisted, and Rukhsana laughed sheepishly, and gulped down the rest of her tea. Then she left, explaining that she had promised to ring home and needed to get a place in the phone queue downstairs.

After she had gone, Yasmin continued reading Baudelaire and found it much easier to concentrate this time. She wasn't quite sure what had catapulted her into saying she would go on Wednesday. But it had something to do with the new light she had begun to see her mother in on the journey down from Sheffield and the fascination that continually drew her after Rukhsana into new and challenging experiences.

The Winnie Mandela Room in the students' union building was a long, draughty room with heavy red velvet curtains along one side, veiling the full-length windows, and concealed lighting on the opposite wall, illuminating faint dusty cobwebs in the grey corners of the ceiling. Tonight the room was also lit by an array of coloured fairy lights strung between the window catches and precariously positioned drawing pins on the other walls. Candles were lit along the tables where the food had been set out in white and green crockery borrowed from the canteen, on red paper tablecloths. Classical Indian sitar and tabla music was playing from a sound system with enormous speakers and coloured lights, and there was a scent of sandalwood incense in the air.

When Rukhsana and Yasmin arrived the room was already full and humming with conversation and laughter. Yasmin was struck by the brilliance of the colours the women were wearing and she decided, with satisfaction, that she had been right to choose something bright herself. She was wearing a turquoise-green silk top and baggy cotton trousers, heavily patterned in turquoise, mauve and black. She had been trying to decide what to wear since four o'clock, when she had rushed home from a conversation class, catching the bus rather than walking. She had tried on most of her wardrobe and refused to allow herself to ask Rukhsana, but had been delighted when Rukhsana expressed total admiration and asked where she bought the trousers. Now she felt nervous again and very self-conscious. Most of the women students seemed to be in saris or suits like Rukhsana, who was wearing a dazzling cerise-pink shalwar kameez with black piping, the kameez flared outwards in a wide skirt and swirled as she turned. Even Atiya, whom Yasmin had never seen out of her jeans and black jacket, was dressed in a long, elegant red and green kurta with tight green

87

pyjamas and a gold-embroidered red dupatta draped over one shoulder. Yasmin noticed some Chinese women in dazzling silk clothes and she saw that the men were mostly in shirts and trousers, but some were also in shalwar kameez of thick buff or grey cotton, and others wore turbans in striking colours. There were plenty of guests, including a group of African students in full African robes and a few white students, here and there, amongst whom Yasmin recognised some other first years.

Yasmin and Rukhsana made their way across the room to where Manjula and Shahnaz were talking to two men. Rukhsana seemed to know everyone and was stopped two or three times in their progress across the room to exchange news and introduce Yasmin. When they reached the far corner they were greeted enthusiastically.

"Hello, Rukhsana!"

"Yasmin! It's great to see you here, how are you doing? Meet Sajid and Ashok. You two, this is Yasmin, she's just started in the first year."

"Hi! Can I get you a drink?" Sajid offered, while Ashok complimented Rukhsana on the lighting with a meaningful look. Yasmin asked for an orange juice, not knowing if there would be alcohol and not wanting to put her foot in it.

"Hey, Rukhsana," Manjula interrupted. "Talking about the lighting, where's Vikram and is it true about you two?"

"Yes, it is," Rukhsana laughed looking resigned. "I don't know how you lot get to hear things so fast. He'll be here later, he had to sort out the fireworks."

"You're a sly one," Manjula teased her. "Never saying a word to anyone. Did you know about this, Yasmin?"

"Er, well, not really," Yasmin blustered, looking at Rukhsana helplessly, but Rukhsana had already turned away to speak to Shahnaz.

"Well, who's going to start the food?" she was saying, "there's no use letting it get cold."

"We were waiting for you," Ashok told her. "We thought someone from the organising committee ought to say a few words. You know, open the proceedings or whatever and we knew you'd do it."

"Oh no, forget it!" Rukhsana replied horrified.

"Oh, go on, Rukhsana, you're really good at that sort of thing," Manjula urged, "Ashok'll chip in if you get stuck."

"'Course I will," Ashok agreed. "But I think a woman should do it."

"Oh, very convenient!" Rukhsana mocked. "Since when have you been interested in women's rights?" But she allowed herself to be led to the end of the room, where Ashok turned the music down and banged a spoon on a table. Rukhsana cleared her throat and Yasmin felt a hollow sinking in her stomach as the room fell silent.

"I'd just like to welcome you all to our modest little celebration for Diwali," Rukhsana began, smiling calmly, her voice sounded even but Yasmin could detect a faint tremor, "Diwali, the Festival of Lights, is a very important and happy festival celebrated by Hindus and Sikhs across the world. In the Asian Society we try to honour each other's festivals and holy days and celebrate whatever is particular to our different cultures and religions, but we never forget the very important things that bind us together as Asian students and as members of the wider black community in this country.

"I'd like to remind all the Asian students here that we have weekly meetings of the Asian Students' Society every Wednesday at seven-thirty in Meeting Room 2 downstairs and you're all very welcome to attend. As well as organising celebrations like this, we also try to educate ourselves about important issues affecting the Asian continent and Asian people in Britain today, and we try to learn more about our own history. We have guest speakers and organise our own seminars to share our skills and knowledge. We also make links with other Asian and black organisations in the city to show our solidarity in the struggle against racism and discrimination," she paused for a moment and Yasmin felt a rush of affection and pride.

"Many of you will know that in India and a lot of other

countries Diwali is celebrated by three days of parties and fireworks and I've heard you can't sleep for the noise of the firecrackers and the flashing of the fireworks. Well, we can't match that here, but we have organised our own little display, with the extremely reluctant permission of the porters, and that will be starting at nine o'clock outside the lower refectory." There was a ripple of applause and cheering across the room. "We hope you all have a very good time and please do help yourselves to all the food that's been prepared for you, I know the cooks would be furious if you let it get cold."

More applause erupted and there was a gentle surge towards the tables. Ashok turned up the volume on the sound system and the buzz of conversation rose in an accompanying crescendo 'till it had reached its former pitch. Rukhsana shrank back into the crowd and joined Yasmin.

"You didn't tell me you could speak so well in public!" Yasmin exclaimed. "You were so good! My mind just goes blank in situations like that."

"But I didn't say anything special," Rukhsana demurred. "Come on, let's get some food," and she led Yasmim over to the tables. There Sajid tracked her down with her orange juice and they chatted for a while about how she found the university.

"This is my second year," he said, "I like it better out of hall, but it's easier to make friends in hall when you first come, isn't it? Aapne kuch khanna hai?"

"I'm sorry," Yasmin apologised in embarrassment, "I don't speak Urdu."

"No apology needed, I just assumed, it's my fault. Do you want something to eat before these lot wolf everything? Here, grab a plate." They helped themselves to biryani and various curries and spoonfuls of green salad and dahi raita, and then moved to a couple of chairs still free by the wall.

"But you are Pakistani, aren't you?" Sajid persisted, when they were sitting down.

"My Dad was. My Mum's English, she brought me up."

"I see, that's why you don't speak Urdu but you recognise it, don't you?"

"Rukhsana's doing, I think. She teaches me odd words, here and there."

"Well, if you ever want any lessons, I'd be happy to oblige," Sajid offered eagerly. Yasmin smiled but did not reply, not knowing what to say.

"You see the man in the green shirt over there, next to the speaker," Sajid pointed out. "Arif, he's like you, mixed race, his Mum's white, but she's a Muslim now. And that girl in the black dress talking to Atiya, she's Anglo-Indian, which is a bit different, her family have been Anglo-Indians for generations, but originally they were the same as you, she comes to our group sometimes. So does Arif."

Yasmin looked at the man talking animatedly on the other side of the room to two African students. She would never have picked him out as any different from the other Asian men, but now she thought she saw a lightness in his skin, maybe, and something in his features. It was strange to have him pointed out, she wondered if anyone had pointed her out to him, and whether he thought she looked English or Asian.

Sajid had moved on to talk about eating places he could recommend in town and Yasmin wondered if he was working round to asking her out for a meal with him. She was quite glad to be interrupted by Rukhsana pulling gently on her sleeve and saying, "Yasmin, sorry to butt in, but I just want to introduce you to Vikram."

Yasmin turned to face a tall, lean man in a pale pink shirt and a thin expensive-looking leather tie. His black hair was cropped short and combed back and his dark eyes smiled humorously above high cheekbones and a slightly arrogant nose.

"Hello, Yasmin," he smiled. "Hope you're enjoying yourself."

"Yes, it's a really good party, you missed Rukhsana's speech," Yasmin replied, fascinated to see the person Rukhsana had been dreaming about. He was very suave and attractive and she could see how happy and excited

Rukhsana was, but she felt a twinge of instinctive suspicion, which she tried to dismiss.

"I've seen it all before, very boring!" Vikram pretended to yawn and Rukhsana poked him in the ribs. "Ow! No, actually, I was busy with other things. Following Rukhsana's instructions, you see, she makes us all work so hard!"

"I wish I could. Not you, I mean all them lot," Rukhsana gestured generally to the rest of the room. "They're happy enough to come to a party, but they'll run a mile if you suggest doing anything serious, like talk about racism, for instance, or child labour in South Asia."

Yasmin felt slightly guilty at the anger in Rukhsana's voice, thinking of the times when she avoided such topics with Rukhsana herself.

"Hey, steady on," Vikram cautioned. "They're not responsible for it, remember. We all have to put up with racism, but we don't have to come to meetings about it as well. Not unless we want to."

"I know, I know," Rukhsana sighed. "It just makes me mad sometimes. I bet hardly anyone comes next week when we want to talk about doing something in the local campaign against racial attacks, they think we're just a social club and that's good enough."

"Well, I'll be there, so that's at least two of us, could be cosy!" Vikram teased, putting his arm round her.

"Behave!" Rukhsana laughed, sliding out again. "You'll embarrass me! Oh, look, they've started dancing. Vikram go and dance, you love showing off!"

Yasmin looked round to see a circle of men dancing in the middle of the room to loud, pulsing bhangra music. Vikram went off obediently to join them, and Yasmin and Rukhsana helped themselves to burfi and gulab jamun and found a corner to sit in, from where Rukhsana pointed out interesting people and Yasmin quizzed her about Vikram.

The party moved out to watch the firework display for a while and when they all drifted back into the Winnie Mandela Room, the volume on the speakers had been turned up and flashing disco lights were playing across the floor. Yasmin and Rukhsana were soon coaxed out of their corner by Shahnaz and Manjula, who dragged them over to the area cleared for dancing.

"Come on Rukhsana, it's Sangeeta. You've got to dance to this," Shahnaz insisted, overriding Rukhsana's loud protests. Yasmin and Manjula watched the two of them mingle with some other women, swirling and twisting, their hands flashing in stylised movements and their feet darting energetically across the floor as music blasted from the great throbbing speakers.

"God, I couldn't do that in a million years, it looks really hard," Yasmin cried out, full of admiration.

"Rubbish! Get some of this down you and you'll soon feel like it!" Manjula encouraged, and she poured some wine from her glass into Yasmin's empty plastic cup. But, before Yasmin could take a sip, Rukhsana had caught her hand and was pulling her into a space on the polished floor.

"But I don't know what to do!" she wailed in horror.

"Just follow me!" Rukhsana shouted above the music, and she began dancing again.

Yasmin moved hesitantly after her, conscious of the great expanse of empty floor around her and the ranks of eyes she imagined watching her. But when she looked up she saw that people were busy dancing themselves, or were immersed in animated conversations by the food tables, and she began to relax and move with the wild, boisterous beat of the music, caught up in a whirl of movement as she watched Rukhsana flying round. She could not follow her hand movements very easily but she improvised ones of her own and soon became lost in the matchless pleasure of expressing the music through her body, feeling herself become part of the flashing iridescent lights and the shrill, feverish, impassioned song flowing and eddying above the insistent bhangra beat. They danced until they were exhausted and breathless, and retreated to some chairs by the window. Yasmin fetched some more orange, a whole carton this time, and two more cups, and they quenched their thirst and went straight back again, joining a large group of their friends laughing and shouting and wheeling round each other in dizzying circles.

By the end of the evening Yasmin was flushed and exhausted, but feeling wildly excited and elated. She kept repeating to Rukhsana how glad she was she had come, as they helped to clear away the discarded plastic plates and cups.

"If you two come now, I'll give you a lift home," Vikram called across the room to them as they scrunched up the torn paper tablecovers and shoved them into a black dustbin liner.

"But we can't just leave Manju and Asha," Rukhsana protested. "Can't you wait?"

"You two go, there's plenty of us left and I'll take the others home in the minibus," Ashok urged from the corner where he was unplugging the speakers. Reluctantly, Rukhsana left the clearing up and Yasmin followed her, deciding it was for Rukhsana and Vikram to sort out, but she thought they should all have stayed to the end.

Vikram drove them back to their hall in his sputtering old Cortina. When they arrived, Yasmin said good-bye and left Rukhsana with Vikram in the car while she went up to her room alone, realising that things were going to be different for her as well now that Rukhsana and Vikram were going out together.

8

CONVERSATIONS

About a week after the party Yasmin called on Sharon late on a dull, misty November afternoon. She had hardly seen her that week and was looking forward to catching up with her and maybe spending an hour or two in meandering conversation. She hurried along the corridor, feeling warm and cheerful with the anticipation of surprising her friend, and knocked briskly on the door. Sharon opened it in a pair of old slippers, a pen in her hand, and soft husky strains of jazz music wafting into the corridor from the record player perched on an upturned wooden crate by her bed.

"Hello, Yasmin!" she exclaimed surprised. "What are you doing over here? Come in."

"Just thought I'd call round. Hope you're not too busy?" Yasmin smiled casually.

"'Course not. You've rescued me from the most boring translation ever set in this university, all about the Retail Price Index! Please stay all afternoon!" Sharon pleaded jokingly, moving to close the door behind Yasmin.

"I'd love to, but I'll have to rush back to do one myself in a bit," Yasmin laughed. "I'm really behind with my work, I've been doing so much else, and going home for the weekend didn't help either." She walked over to the window seat, which Sharon had covered in a thick blue and green blanket, and sat on the edge of the seat, watching Sharon fill the kettle.

"So, how are you?" she asked, raising her voice slightly above the music.

"I'm fine," Sharon smiled. "Loads of work, of course, and Trish is having boyfriend trouble, but apart from that everything's great."

"Oh? What's happened?"

"It started with Steve getting really jealous because he said Trish was flirting with Duncan and of course Duncan backed him up and acted the innocent. Then Trish found out Steve's still seeing this girl in Norwich that he's been going out with for years, so of course Trish got really upset. But now it all seems to be okay again. I don't know..." Sharon's voice trailed off wearily.

"You sound a bit fed up of it all," Yasmin suggested sympathetically.

"I just never know where I am with her," Sharon replied, in exasperation. "One minute Steve's the biggest monster out, and the next she won't hear a word against him and they're pretending nothing ever happened. I've had enough of traumas at home without staying up all night here sorting them out."

"So you get to hear all the gory details?" Yasmin prompted, secretly enjoying Sharon's annoyance with Trish.

"Only the bad bits, when there's a good patch I hardly see her for days, she's too busy being in love," Sharon muttered, bitterly, and she handed Yasmin a mug of strong tea.

"Thanks. I know what you mean, I don't see so much of Rukhsana now she's going out with Vikram. We used to just bump into each other all the time on the corridor, but now she's always staying over at Atiya's house in town because Vikram lives down the road."

"I thought you went around with her all the time," Sharon contradicted. "I heard you went to that party they had in the union last week, the one with the fireworks."

"The Diwali Party?"

"Yeah, I didn't know it was your sort of thing. You said before you didn't know anything about it?"

"I didn't," Yasmin replied. "But I think I'd like to now. I went to one of the Asian Society meetings last night as well, it was really interesting."

"Can anyone go, then?"

"Not usually. I mean, it's a society for Asian students, like it says," Yasmin replied, uneasily, feeling precarious about her own position.

"That's a bit elitist, isn't it?" Sharon pursued, she leaned back in her chair and Yasmin sensed a hint of anger in her voice.

"They do have open meetings as well, like the party, or if there's a speaker from outside," she argued defensively. "I don't think there's anything wrong in a group having some meetings just for itself."

"So what do they talk about that's so interesting?"

"Oh, all sorts of things," Yasmin replied evasively, knowing that Rukhsana would not like her to be talking to Sharon about their meetings. "You know, things about Asia and about Asian people in this country..."

"Don't they think it's a bit funny you going. I mean, you might have divided loyalties, mightn't you? You could be a spy," Sharon teased, but it seemed to Yasmin she was only half joking.

"Don't be silly," Yasmin forced a laugh. "We don't have to swear allegiance or anything. It's not a secret society, you know. Everyone's been really welcoming and they want me to join if I like it."

"Sounds like you already have! No wonder we never see you," Sharon said grumpily.

"I've just been busy with work, that's all," Yasmin insisted. "I've been planning this games evening for the youth club tonight with Ben, it took much more organising than we thought. Anyway, I came round to see if you want to go out at the weekend."

"Oh yes, definitely. If you can spare the time," Sharon said in a tone of heavy sarcasm.

"I've come to see you now, haven't I?" Yasmin responded sharply. "And I'm asking you if you want to go out."

"Okay, okay, what about tomorrow night?" Sharon replied quickly.

Yasmin looked uncomfortable,

"I'm afraid I'm busy tomorrow," she admitted awkwardly, "I'm going to eat at Atiya's with Rukhsana, and I think we're getting a video out later on. I was thinking of Saturday or Sunday really."

"I'm going out for a drink with Fiona and this other friend of her's on Saturday night, you could come too?"

"Okay," Yasmin agreed. "Maybe we could have lunch sometime next week, just you and me? Anyway, I'd better get on. Seeing you with that translation is making me nervous about all the work I've got to do," and she rose to leave.

She walked back across the campus through the early dusk, shivering as the chill night fog curled in across the wet grass and circled the yellow street lamps in blurred halos. Her visit had not been what she expected, but she was satisfied that they had arranged something for the weekend, and maybe Sharon had just been in a bad mood because of Trish. Yasmin felt slightly guilty for not going to see her sooner, but she told herself Sharon could have come across to visit her just as easily. Putting the conversation to the back of her mind, she turned her thoughts to the evening ahead and getting herself organised before going out to the youth club.

She was busy working on the first page of her French translation, just after six o'clock, when she was interrupted by a loud knock at the door. She opened it to a breathless student she hardly recognised.

"Your Mum's on the phone downstairs!"

Yasmin grabbed her keys and hurried down to the phone on the ground floor, remembering that she had meant to phone at the weekend, but kept postponing it, telling herself it would be nicer to write. The letter she had started was still in her medieval language file half-finished, it was stuck at the part explaining the Diwali party and she was still waiting for inspiration to carry it forward.

She calmed her breath for a moment and then picked up the receiver lying on a small shelf under the grey semi-circular hood of the phone booth.

"Hello, Mum!" she cried breezily, her eye wandering over the instruction board scrawled with graffiti and cryptic messages.

"Yasmin! Why haven't we heard from you for so long? I was worried about you."

Yasmin felt deeply guilty at her anxious tone. "I know, I'm really sorry, I was just busy. I started a letter, but it never got finished, and I kept meaning to phone, but it's hard to get a phone free when you want one," she apologised lamely.

"Never mind. Are you all right, though? I thought you might be upset after what we talked about that Saturday."

"Oh no, nothing like that, you mustn't worry about me," Yasmin reassured her dismayed, "I'm fine, honestly. And thanks for your letters, I will write back properly, it's just I've had loads of work on recently and I've been out a lot as well."

"Well, if you're sure you're all right, I'll try not to worry," Maggie said doubtfully. "It's easier said than done, you know, you'll understand one day. Anyway, I'm glad you've been enjoying yourself. So, tell me what's been happening, I want to hear all about it."

"Oh, nothing special," Yasmin replied, wondering where to start. "Just the usual, you know, films and the youth club, and I went to the union disco last Saturday with some people from my course."

"Oh yes? How's Sharon?"

"She didn't come on Saturday, actually, but I saw her today and she was fine."

"Is everything all right for her at home, then?"

"I think so, she didn't mention it, so it must be," Yasmin replied, realising she hadn't picked up on Sharon's comment about traumas at home.

"Have you asked her yet about coming to stay at Christmas?"

"Well, no, actually, I was thinking of inviting Rukhsana, if that's all right with you? She's going to stay on a bit in the holidays and she was saying the other day how she hates the first weekend when everyone else goes home, so I thought she could come home with me for a couple of days."

"Oh, I see," said Maggie slowly, then, rallying. "Of course, you invite whoever you want, love. You must tell me what she likes nearer the time, eh? And if there's anything special you two want to do. Is she your best friend now?"

"Yes, I suppose she is. I know what you said about her leaving and everything, but she might stay on after her degree and anyway I can't help it if I get on best with her."

"No, of course you can't, I'm sure she's a very good friend. I'm not criticising, you know."

"I know," Yasmin laughed relaxing a little.

"So, what else have you been doing?" Maggie prompted.

"Rukhsana and I went to a party last week, for Diwali. You know, the Hindu festival? The Asian Students' Society put it on."

"Are you sure you haven't been brooding?" Maggie interrupted anxiously. "It doesn't do any good thinking about the past and your Father all the time, you know."

"Of course I'm not brooding," Yasmin insisted, sighing. "I went to a party and enjoyed myself, what's that got to do with brooding? Mum, will you stop worrying?"

"All right, you just make sure you tell me if anything's wrong. Anyway, aren't we going to see you again before the holidays? What about the weekend after this?"

"I can't, I'm afraid. I'm going home with Rukhsana that weekend. She invited me last week, and after that it's only three weeks 'till the end of term, so I might as well wait 'till I come back for the holidays."

"Oh dear, so we're not going to see you 'till the holidays," Maggie repeated subdued. "That's a pity. I hope it's all right with Rukhsana's mother for you to go and stay. Are they a big family?"

"Yes, but they're not all at home, her big sister's just got married and one of her brothers is at Newcastle Polytechnic. They all sound really nice, I'm looking forward to it."

"Well, I hope you have a lovely time, it's very nice of

Rukhsana to invite you. What are you doing this weekend?"

"Working mostly, I'm really behind. But I'm going out for a drink with Sharon on Saturday, and tomorrow night I'm going for a meal at Rukhsana's friends' house. What about you?"

"Rod's working on Saturday, he's taking a minibus trip out into Derbyshire, rock climbing or something equally ridiculous for this time of year. So I thought I'd take the car and go over to Joan and Michael's, get it over with before it gets too near Christmas and they're tempted to start all that Christmas present stuff again."

"Good idea. Look, I've got to go now Mum, but I'll finish that letter this weekend, I promise."

"Don't worry about it, love, just keep in touch and look after yourself, okay?"

"Okay, love to Rod. 'Bye for now!"

"Bye, love."

Yasmin put the phone down, frowning thoughtfully, and walked away past the queue that had formed in the corridor, as another student leapt forward to occupy her phone booth.

The union bar was packed and noisy by the time Yasmin and Ben reached it later that evening. They had stayed on at the youth club to tidy up after their highly successful games session, and then walked over to the students' union for a drink before catching the last bus back to their halls. Usually Maureen and Hilary, came too, but tonight they had gone on to a pub to meet their own friends, and Yasmin was quite looking forward to talking to Ben on his own. She had really enjoyed talking to him the week before when Maureen and Hilary had gone off to play pool for half an hour, she found him a very interesting person.

By the time they reached the union they were both exhausted, but feeling very happy and satisfied with their evening's work.

"Mmm...just what I needed. I'm shattered," Yasmin

sighed, taking a long sip from her glass of cider and leaning back against the worn vinyl seat-back. Ben drew up a stool on the other side of the table and dumped his jacket on the floor. He was thin and angular with a long elegant face and thick dark curly hair, a pair of round wire-rimmed glasses perched on the bridge of his nose and he had a wry, quizzical smile.

"Me too. I won't be doing that again in a hurry," he agreed, with feeling. "It was fun though, and they all enjoyed it."

"Oh yes, so did I. It's a pity I won't be here for the Christmas party."

"Are you going straight off at the end of term?"

"Yes, I've told Mum now, and Rukhsansa's coming home with me that weekend. I think I'll be ready to go home by then, anyway."

"I don't think I'm ever ready to go home," Ben said gloomily. "In fact, you're the only person I know who gets on with their parents, sorry, parent. Most of us are dreading going back for Christmas and we'll put it off as long as possible."

"I know, some people thought I was weird going home for the weekend," Yasmin laughed. "But my Mum's great and I like Sheffield. I bet you like your family really, you just say you don't because everyone else does, it's supposed to be cool to hate your parents, isn't it?"

"I suppose so," Ben laughed grudgingly. "They're okay, so far. They're very proud of me getting on a law course and everything, but it only lasts as long as I'm doing what they want. It's all very conditional, you see, and I know now I'm not going to measure up in the end."

"I don't see why you say that," Yasmin argued, puzzled.

"No, well I can't explain, that's just how it is," he said enigmatically. "Anyway, how did your Asian Society meeting go last night?"

"Really good," Yasmin replied enthusiastically. "It was very interesting and I knew lots of people already so I felt fine. It made me think a lot, in fact I think it's still sinking in. Rukhsana was brilliant, as usual, she knows so much and she's really good at putting things in perspective."

"You really like her, don't you?" Ben commented, curiously.

"Of course, she's my best friend - and she understands loads about politics and how things have got to be like they are."

"She's had two years away from home to sort things out. Maybe we'll be like that when we're finalists."

"I don't think I will be," Yasmin said doubtfully. "I make such a meal out of sorting out what I think about the simplest things, like all that fuss I made last week trying to decide whether or not to go to the meeting, you must have been bored stiff listening to it all."

"Not at all," Ben assured her, looking serious. "Listen, you're doing great at sorting things out, at least you're honest about it, take it from me, I know what I'm talking about!"

Yasmin looked at him curiously and he looked down at the beer mat he was digging into the table and frowned.

"And?" she said expectantly.

"And what?" he retorted.

"Well, what is it that you haven't sorted out then?"

"Everything, but it's too complicated to go into now," he sighed, and then he looked up brightly and said, "Do you want another drink?"

"Yes, but I'll get them. Same again?" Yasmin replied, getting up and Ben nodded, handing her his glass.

She struggled through the crowd to the bar and squeezed in between a tall man in a black leather jacket just paying for his drinks, and a woman in a dazzling green dress, who gave her a quick comradely glance as they both leaned forward to catch the bar tender's eye. As the man backed away from the bar, nursing his drinks, Yasmin was aware of someone else slipping in beside her and was startled to hear her name spoken right by her ear. She looked round to see Vikram close beside her, laughing at her surprise.

"Hello!" she cried. "What are you doing here? Is Rukhsana with you?"

"Good grief, no!" he replied in mock horror. "She doesn't go to bars, you know that. I'm with Ashok and some other friends. Look, you'd better order." They paused while Yasmin ordered and then Vikram said, "Who are you with, then?"

"Ben he's over there, sitting down, in the black jumper. We help out at a youth club near here on Thursday nights," Yasmin explained.

Vikram looked across the room at Ben, who was staring absently at the flashing display on the slot machine near their table.

"First year?" Vikram asked frowning critically, and when Yasmin nodded he said, "Yes, he looks a bit young, is he Jewish?"

"I haven't the faintest idea!" Yasmin replied, astonished at the question. "He never said so."

"He looks like he might be. You could do better, Yasmin."

"Hey! We're just friends!" Yasmin laughed indignantly, as she took her change and picked up her drinks. "He's very nice, why don't you come across and say hello?"

"Another time," Vikram declined. "I've got thirsty friends waiting. I'll see you around."

"See you," Yasmin replied and eased her way out of the crush by the bar, a drink in each hand, not knowing whether to be amused or angry with Vikram.

When she got back to her seat she told Ben she had met Rukhsana's boyfriend at the bar.

"He asked if you were Jewish," she said tentatively.

"Did he now?" Ben smiled ironically. "How clever of him, well, he's right, of course. It's one of those things I'm not very sorted out about, I'm afraid."

"Don't be afraid," Yasmin reproached him warmly. "You should know I understand, we must both be as mixed up as each other about who we are!"

"Yes, I suppose so," Ben spoke slowly and looked at her as if trying to weigh something up. "We are friends, aren't we?"

"Of course," Yasmin replied emphatically. She was

beginning to feel a little nervous, the conversation suddenly seemed to be getting very heavy. Ben gulped down another mouthful of beer and cleared his throat.

"I feel bad with you being so open about everything," he began, as if repeating words he had been rehearsing all evening. "You see, there's something I haven't told you. Well, I haven't told anyone here, actually. I'd like to tell you, I think you might know anyway..."

`Oh God,' she thought, `he's going to ask me out.'

"Say it, Ben!" she pleaded. "The suspense is killing me!"

He laughed apologetically and, taking a deep breath, said quietly, "I'm gay."

Yasmin was thrown. She felt her mind go unhelpfully blank as she tried to comprehend what that meant to her.

"I don't know what to say," she blurted out honestly. "You're the first gay person I've ever met."

"Don't be so sure!" Ben interrupted. "I'm the first person who's ever told you they're gay, that's all."

"Okay," Yasmin assented. Looking at him, she realised, that her overriding feeling was one of disappointment that he would not be asking her out after all, she liked him more than she had admitted to herself. Apart from that, she could not quite identify what she felt.

"Well, what do you think?" he asked impatiently.

"Nothing really. I mean, it doesn't make any difference to anything, does it?" Yasmin said hesitantly.

"It makes a difference to me," Ben responded passionately. It's who I am, like you're Asian, or whatever you decide to be in the end. To me, it changes everything."

"I know. I didn't mean it doesn't matter, give us a chance!" Yasmin exclaimed and Ben smiled sheepishly.

"I just meant it doesn't change us being friends, or doing the youth club, or any of that," she continued, watching his face carefully. "I think it's fine, it's great, in fact, maybe it's the reason you're such a nice man!"

They both laughed, looking at each other with shy embarrassment, and Ben breathed out loudly, saying, "Phew! That was really terrifying, now I've only got the other ninety-nine people I know to tell!"

"Have you really not told any of your friends?" Yasmin asked amazed.

"Certainly not!" he said. "You don't know what it's like, they're all so macho, I'd be crucified."

"But there must be other gay men around?"

"And they all keep their heads down, like me," Ben said firmly. "How many lesbians do you know about in this place?"

"None," Yasmin admitted, quickly sifting through all the women students she knew in her head.

"Which doesn't mean there aren't any, it just means they haven't told you about themselves," Ben pointed out.

"But there's a Gaysoc, they had a stall at Freshers' Fair."

"I know," Ben admitted miserably. "That's why I think you're so brave, going to your meeting last night, I've been dithering about Gaysoc all term."

"Oh, honestly, after all the things you said to me last week! `You'll feel much better,' you said, `if you don't like it you don't have to go again'...what a fraud!" Yasmin teased, laughing as he shrugged his shoulders helplessly. "Just GO, you silly!"

"Well, maybe I will," Ben agreed, smiling grudgingly. "I don't suppose I'll hear the end of it now, will I?"

"No you won't," Yasmin replied, looking at him affectionately. She decided she could easily live with him not falling in love with her, she really liked their friendship as it was.

They chatted on for another half an hour about lighter things, 'till they both felt completely relaxed again, and then wandered down to the bus stop and caught the bus home. As they parted by the entrance to Yasmin's hall, Ben said, anxiously, "You won't tell anyone, will you? I mean, not even someone you trust like Rukhsana. It's absolutely private between you and me, okay?"

"Of course, I promise," Yasmin reassured him. "See you next week, and I expect you to have done something about Gaysoc!"

Ben laughed and jogged off down the path towards his

hall.

Yasmin went in and climbed the stairs to her floor slowly, thinking about how a few words can change how everything appears. She wondered why Ben had chosen to tell her, out of all the people he knew, she didn't really understand, but she was quite flattered.

She forgot all about her encounter with Vikram until she met him again the following week coming out of the university library as she was going in. He beamed broadly when he saw her and caught her arm excitedly. "Yasmin! Just the person I wanted to see! Come and have a coffee, I want to talk to you."

"Not now, Vikram, I'm really behind for this essay on Friday," Yasmin replied, squirming uncomfortably and quietly removing her arm from his grip.

"Oh, but it'll only take a few minutes, we could go to the snack bar in the Arts Block and you'll be back here in fifteen minutes, please," he pleaded, trying to look mournful.

Yasmin hesitated and then, shrugging her shoulders with a resigned smile, she said, "Okay, but it'll have to be quick, I've got loads of reading to do."

They hurried over to the Arts Block, Vikram chatting jovially about how cold his shared house was and how he and his friends sneaked into their old halls to have baths and showers. Yasmin said very little, feeling slightly pressured into having this cup of coffee and wondering what he wanted to talk about.

When Vikram had bought their coffees and they had settled themselves at a small table by the long first floor window overlooking the car park, he smiled at her, warmly. "So, Yasmin, how's life treating you?"

"Fine," Yasmin replied non-committally.

"Seen any more of that friend of yours?"

"Not since last week, if it's any of your business. I told you, I only see him on Thursdays at the youth club," Yasmin said impatiently.

"I'm only asking because you're Rukhsana's friend and I

care about you," Vikram said earnestly, leaning forward and looking seriously into her eyes. "I know Rukhsana worries about you too, we don't want you to get hurt."

"Well thanks, but Ben won't hurt me," Yasmin said confidently, feeling deeply irritated by the way he was drawing Rukhsana into the conversation.

"Look, I've been here a lot longer than you, and I know how some of these white students take advantage of our girls, they're very clever and know all the right things to say to put you off your guard."

"He's Jewish, as you pointed out yourself, and I can take care of myself, thank you, I have been out with boys before," Yasmin interrupted crossly.

"So you are going out with him?" Vikram leapt in quickly. Yasmin thought about saying yes just to spite him, but decided it would only provoke him to a further lecture and she now wanted to get away as soon as possible, she didn't like the way this conversation was going at all.

"No, I'm not and I won't ever be," she said shortly. "Look, I don't want to have an argument, it would only upset Rukhsana, so if there's nothing else, I'll get back to the library."

"Now you're cross with me," Vikram said sadly. "I'm sorry, Yasmin, I was only trying to help."

"I'm not cross," Yasmin sighed, "I just don't think it's anyone else's business who I go for a drink with in the union."

"Of course it isn't, I was out of order," Vikram agreed humbly and leaning across the table, he put his hand over Yasmin's and said, softly, "I just want to see you with someone who'll respect you and treat you right."

Yasmin flinched and tried to draw her hand back, but he pressed harder and continued, "I do care about you, you know, I want you to remember that."

She could feel his breath on her cheek as she looked to the side to avoid his eyes. Then he slowly released his hold and she snatched her hand away and put it in her lap, feeling slightly shocked. She looked hard at the table, trying to gather her thoughts, she could still feel the ugly, insistent pressure of his hand and smell the hot sourness of his breath.

"There was something else," Vikram said calmly, tilting his chair back, "I'm inviting you and Rukhsana to dinner at our house, after you get back from visiting her parents. Rukhsana said next Tuesday's okay for her, how would that suit you?"

"Fine," Yasmin replied, wishing she had never come for this drink.

"Good. Half-past seven, then. I've invited Sajid as well, he usually comes round on a Tuesday. Should be a nice evening."

"Right, well I'd better go," Yasmin said briskly, rising from her seat and lifting her jacket off the back of the chair.

"Oh, one more thing, don't tell Rukhsana I put my foot in it about your friend, will you? She'll only be cross with me for interfering," Vikram suggested, casually, not moving from his seat.

"All right," Yasmin agreed hurriedly. "I must go, see you." She walked away quickly without looking back, feeling angry and ashamed and seething inside. `Who does he think he is?' she thought, furiously, `my own mother doesn't tell me who I can and can't see and I know what this dinner's about, it's to fix me up with Sajid, well he can forget that.'

"Hello Yasmin," a voice called out, and Yasmin looked up to see Atiya by the entrance to the snack bar.

"Oh, hello," she smiled weakly.

"You're in a hurry," Atiya said. "Have you seen Shahnaz in there? She said she'd meet me here ten minutes ago, but I was late."

"No," Yasmin replied guiltily. "But I wasn't looking for anyone. I must get to the library. 'Bye."

"Hope I haven't missed her, see you anyway." Atiya smiled sweetly as Yasmin hurried on, desperate to get away somewhere quiet and anonymous where she could reflect on what had happened.

9

A STRANGE KIND OF HOMECOMING

Yasmin sat demurely on the red velvet sofa in the front room of Rukhsana's parents' house. Rukhsana was in the kitchen, helping her mother with the Friday evening meal. Yasmin had offered to come too, but had been told to relax and drink her tea, which was piping hot and tasted of boiled milk and some sweet, scented spice Rukhsana said was cardamom. She could hear muffled chatter and laughter drifting down the hallway from the kitchen, and upstairs rock music was thumping dully through the floorboards. The room was spotlessly clean and tidy, with a thick red and brown carpet and red sofas along two walls. Along the third wall there was a heavy sideboard covered with a white crocheted cloth, on which a large television and video sat, draped in similar cloths. The black tiled mantelpiece above the gas fire was decorated with small baskets of plastic flowers and framed group photographs of various branches of the family. Above the mantelpiece there was a large mirror and above that a circular copper plaque inscribed with an intricate design of intertwined black letters that Yasmin presumed were in Arabic script. There were similar designs in small gold picture frames mounted in the alcoves on either side of the fireplace, and near the door there hung a photograph of vast throngs of people gathered around a towering tomb-like monument covered in black cloth. On the low coffee table in front of Yasmin, Rukhsana's mother had left a small plate of plain biscuits and another of sliced apple and orange pieces. Yasmin picked at the biscuits as she gazed slowly round the room.

Suddenly the door swung open and a young girl in a pale yellow shalwar kameez and a long ponytail burst into the room.

"Oh!" she stopped abruptly when she saw Yasmin and smiled shyly. "Hello, who are you?"

"Hello," Yasmin laughed. "I'm Rukhsana's friend, Yasmin. Are you Nasrin?"

"How did you know my name?" Nasrin asked her eyes widening in amazement.

"Rukhsana told me, and she told me you're in the last year at junior school now, and you're very clever."

"Oh," Nasrin squirmed still hanging onto the door handle. "Where's Rukhsana?"

"In the kitchen with your Mum, let's go and see what they're doing?" Yasmin suggested, picking up her empty tea cup. She followed Nasrin down the dark hallway to the hot, steamy kitchen where Rukhsana was making chapattis, slapping them from one open palm to another before placing them on the black tawa, where they writhed and puffed up from the heat of the gas flame. Her mother, Shaheen, was stirring a pan full of bubbling curry. She was a large, plump woman with a round face and wrinkles in the soft brown skin across her forehead and around her tired eyes. She smiled kindly at Yasmin and said something to Rukhsana in Punjabi, which Rukhsana answered, laughing.

"She asked me if you're a Hindu because you don't eat meat," Rukhsana explained.

"Don't you speak our language?" Nasrin asked, taking a biscuit from the half-empty packet lying open on a work surface.

"Chup!" her mother reprimanded quickly, then taking Yasmin's cup asked, "Will you have more tea, Yasmin?"

"No thanks," Yasmin declined. "Can I do something? Let me stir the curry."

"No, no," Shaheen insisted. "You go and sit in the other room. Nasrin, go with bahji, put the television on."

"Go on," Rukhsana laughed, as Yasmin looked at her helplessly. "You know you're tired, just go and flop!"

Yasmin felt a little cut off, as if Rukhsana had been absorbed back into the very walls of the house, leaving her stranded on the outside.

Nasrin led Yasmin cheerfully back to the front room, where they watched the end of children's television together and then played hangman in the back of a notebook Yasmin kept in her blue canvas shoulder bag. Yasmin studied Nasrin's face with interest. She was strikingly similar to Rukhsana and Yasmin wondered if this was how Rukhsana looked when she was ten. She found the idea fascinating and wondered what it must be like to have brothers and sisters like mirror images of your younger self.

Her thoughts were interrupted by Rukhsana shouting in the hall to whoever was upstairs and the subsequent thump of heavy feet tumbling down the staircase and along the corridor to the kitchen. There followed a busy procession of piles of cutlery, crockery and dishes of food into the front room, which were spread out on the coffee table and over a pink tablecloth laid on the floor in front of the fire. Eventually everyone came in and settled down on the settees, or sat cross-legged on the floor. Yasmin was introduced to Farzana, who was sixteen and apparently responsible for the music upstairs. She was very glamorous in a gold-embroidered blue kameez, with her hair tied tightly in a high ponytail, hanging down her back almost to her waist. She was taller than Rukhsana and had a longer, sharper face, and her hair glinted with auburn tints from frequent henna-ing. Their brother, Shabir, was a gangly fourteen-year-old with a round face like his mother and a croaky, unpredictable voice. After a brief awkward greeting to Yasmin, he sat on the floor with Nasrin and watched the television with total absorption, ignoring everyone else.

"Where's your Dad?" Yasmin asked Rukhsana, serving herself from a large oval dish piled high with biryani rice.

"Has he gone to the mosque, ammi?" Rukhsana turned to her mother.

"No, not this week, he's on late shift. My husband works very hard, Yasmin, he has a long day," Shaheen explained carefully to Yasmin. "And his health is bad."

"He should give up," Rukhsana agreed. "He's not well,

but he won't go to a doctor, our cousin told him once they do experiments on Asians in the hospital."

"That's ridiculous," Farzana interrupted crossly. "He's just paranoid, anyway he could go to an Asian doctor."

"You tell him then," Rukhsana retorted coolly but Farzana ignored her and carried on eating, there was an easy familiarity to their bickering that Yasmin found very soothing.

"This is delicious," she said licking her fingers appreciatively. "I was really hungry."

"Have some more," Shaheen urged, pushing various dishes towards Yasmin. "You must eat more than that."

Yasmin happily spooned more onto her plate and for a while the only sound heard was the television as they all concentrated on their food. Then Shaheen asked Yasmin politely, "Your mother is well?"

"Yes, thank you, very well."

"And your father?"

Yasmin shot an anxious glance at Rukhsana, realising she did not know what had already been said. Rukhsana smiled reassuringly and said, "I told you, ammi, he lives in Pakistan."

"I haven't seen him since I was little, but I think he's all right," Yasmin continued. Shaheen tutted and shook her head sadly.

"Your poor mother, she must be very lonely," she sympathised, "Rukhsana says she's a Christian."

"She's English," Yasmin qualified. "But she's not really a Christian."

"Aren't you a Muslim?" Nasrin interrupted, suddenly turning away from the television as she realised she was missing an interesting adult conversation.

"Mind your own business, Nasrin," Farzana said sharply.

"No, I'm not," Yasmin smiled at Nasrin. "My Dad was a Muslim, but I'm not any religion."

"Not any religion?" Nasrin repeated puzzled. "But you have to be, everyone is."

"No they're not, bozo," Shabir mocked gruffly, without

looking round.

"Leave her alone," Rukhsana intervened protectively, leaning forward and putting an arm round her little sister's shoulders, "She doesn't know."

"But it's true," Nasrin insisted, looking round defiantly. "Isn't it, Rukhsana? Everyone's got to be a Muslim or a Sikh or something, haven't they?"

"Well, actually, no," Rukhsana admitted softly. "Lots of people don't believe in any religion."

Nasrin looked disappointed and Yasmin began to feel uncomfortably like some sort of freak.

"So who is going to find you a husband?" Shaheen asked Yasmin, looking perturbed.

"I don't think anyone is," Yasmin replied cautiously. "I don't know if I'll be getting married."

"Oh dear," Shaheen said disapprovingly. "You must get married, or you will be lonely like your mother."

"I think Yasmin's mother is very happy," Rukhsana interrupted firmly. "She has a good job, her own house, and she can do what she wants, you don't have to be married to be happy."

"Maybe not for an English lady, but for us, yes," Shaheen responded, looking at Rukhsana sternly and then she turned to Yasmin and said brightly, "How are your studies, Yasmin?"

"Oh, fine," Yasmin smiled, quickly adjusting to the change of mood. "There's always too much work to do, but I try my best."

"Rukhsana says your rooms are next door."

"Practically, yes."

"So, do you go out together too?"

"Yes, quite often," Yasmin caught Rukhsana's cautioning gaze. "Sometimes we go to eat with Atiya and Shahnaz, I think you've met them? Or we go to the art gallery or a museum. In the evenings we mostly work, especially Rukhsana, she's so busy now with Finals."

"I know," Shaheen sighed fondly. "She always works too hard, too many figures, you'll spoil your eyes, beti."

"Do you wear a shalwar kameez?" Nasrin piped up, still

trying to understand where Yasmin fitted into her world.

"Not really," Yasmin replied, slightly embarrassed.

"You should. It would suit you, why don't you try one of mine?" Farzana said enthusiastically. "Wouldn't she look good, Rukhsana?"

Rukhsana smiled, but said nothing.

"I have tried some of Rukhsana's suits," Yasmin admitted. "They're very nice, but I think Rukhsana looks better in them."

"Oh, wear one tonight, please," Nasrin pleaded excitedly. "Just for us, promise you will."

"Well, I'll try one on if you like," Yasmin agreed reluctantly. "Later on, okay?"

"Now!" Nasrin insisted pulling her arm gently.

"Nasrin," Shaheen interrupted, in tones of dire warning, "Leave bahji alone, she's tired. Off the television now, Shabir, it's your turn for the dishes." She lifted herself slowly from her seat and began to gather together the plates on the table. Shabir groaned loudly and switched off the television. Then he and Farzana carried the piled plates away, while Rukhsana listened to Nasrin read from the reading book she had brought home from school and Yasmin watched them fascinated. After they had had more tea and pieces of fruit, Rukhsana and Yasmin took their bags upstairs to the room Farzana and Nasrin had temporarily vacated for them.

It was a small sparsely furnished room, with posters of Bombay film stars covering the walls. There were two single beds covered with heavy patterned quilts and a narrow aisle down the centre of the room. By the door there stood a solid wooden chest of drawers. When they were alone, sprawled on their respective beds, Rukhsana said, "Thanks for saying that about us staying in every evening to work."

"I'm not stupid you know," Yasmin replied. "I can see that parties and going out with Vikram are hardly common knowledge. Does anyone know?"

"Not even Farzana, it wouldn't be fair 'cos then she'd have to lie too and it's hard enough for me."

115

"I'd hate to have to lie to my Mum," Yasmin reflected soberly.

"I bet you don't always tell her the whole truth, sometimes people don't really want to know everything anyway," Rukhsana challenged.

Yasmin suddenly remembered that she hadn't said anything to Rukhsana yet about the incident in the cafe with Vikram. She was aware of her silence on the issue as a burden, a kind of barrier between them which she didn't like. It was like the barrier between her and Maggie because she still hadn't told her about the Asian Students' Society meetings or about Ben being gay. But maybe Rukhsana was right, maybe really it would be better if she didn't know, she was so happy with Vikram at the moment, and hearing about that would just upset her. She decided to try and forget about it.

They were both silent for a while, thinking back over the meal in the front room and listening to the familiar noises of the household, pans clattering in the kitchen where Shabir was washing up noisily and resentfully, and a television blaring in the back room next to the kitchen, where Nasrin and Farzana had been sent to watch their soap operas. Yasmin studied Rukhsana's pensive expression.

"You're very quiet at home, aren't you?" she commented.

"I suppose so," Rukhsana agreed. "There's enough noise without me, I just like to sit back and let it all sink in."

"I know what you mean, they're all really nice and your Mum is lovely, she's really proud of you, isn't she?"

"Oh yes, but she's scared that whatever I do is going to influence all the others, I wish I was the youngest, I don't think they'd mind half as much if I didn't get married."

"I see what you mean about getting married, it's not really up for discussion, is it?"

"No, but they know not talking about it isn't going to solve anything," Rukhsana sighed. "I don't know what the big deal is anyway. My aunty Farida never got married, she's my favourite aunty and she's really great. I know my Dad's family all talk about her and her women friends..."

"You mean she's a lesbian?" Yasmin asked, incredulously.

"I think so, no-one's ever told me properly. I think they're scared she might influence me. Anyway, I really like her, she just does what she wants."

"I bet your Mum thinks I'm a bad influence."

"Not at all," Rukhsana laughed. "She knows very well I make my own mistakes, don't you worry about that. She can't quite make you out, but she thinks you're very nice."

At this point Nasrin poked her head round the door and asked tentatively, "Is it time for the shalwar kameez now?"

Yasmin laughed and nodded, and Nasrin rushed off to tell Farzana.

Yasmin found the colours of Farzana's clothes too bright, and in the end she chose a simple fawn-coloured suit of Rukhsana's with brown embroidery around the neckline and the hem of the kameez. Rukhsana also gave her a cluster of thin pearl-inlaid bangles and Nasrin brought some large gold earrings from her mother's bedside table, she was very excited and kept brushing Yasmin's hair and making her turn round. Yasmin began to enjoy herself, she liked the feel of the loose silky material and she could smell the faint scent of jasmine oil that always pervaded Rukhsana's room, trapped in the clothes. Farzana led her into their mother's room where there was a large mirror on the wardrobe door. Yasmin looked at herself shyly, she liked the long elegant lines of the suit and the soft fawn colour against her dark hair and brown skin. To her own surprise she looked relaxed and comfortable. Nasrin stood beside her, fidgeting excitedly, and it occurred to Yasmin that many people, seeing them like this together, would take them for sisters. She stared at herself in amazement, and for a moment saw an ordinary young Asian woman in shalwar kameez. Then the thought of her mother flashed across her mind and the image she saw shifted back to Yasmin dressed in

Rukhsana's clothes.

"Come on, let's go and show ammi," Nasrin urged pulling her arm, and she led Yasmin downstairs triumphantly. Shaheen gave an approving smile when they appeared at the kitchen door.

"Now you look like a proper Pakistani girl," she said with satisfaction. "Very beautiful."

"Wear it all tonight," Nasrin urged, "and tomorrow."

"You can keep the bangles, I've got loads," Rukhsana added.

"I don't know about tomorrow," Yasmin replied thinking she still couldn't see herself going out in such unfamiliar clothes. "But I'll definitely wear it tonight." She followed Nasrin and Rukhsana into the back room, which was obviously the everyday sitting room, while the front room was strictly for visitors. There they all settled down together to watch a video in Urdu about two friends who fall in love with the same woman. They turned the light off so the room was only lit by the dazzling television screen and the orange glow of the gas fire. Rukhsana explained bits of it to Yasmin as they went along and Yasmin picked up the rest from the characters' expressions and the dramatic action. She found it difficult to get into at first, but after a while she got used to the different style and began to feel quite involved.

When Rukhsana's father came home they stopped the video for a while as he greeted them all and Shaheen went to fetch some food. As he sat down he smiled at Yasmin and said politely, "Assalaam alaikum."

Yasmin panicked for a moment, realising it was because of her clothes that he was assuming she would understand, but she remembered that she did know how to reply and said shyly, "Waalaikum salaam."

He then asked her something else which she did not understand and Rukhsana intervened to explain. They all had more food and carried on watching the video in the semi-darkened room. Rukhsana's parents talked in low voices for a little while, looking at Yasmin from time to time, until Rukhsansa said something sharply in Punjabi and then there was silence as the film built to a violent climax.

Yasmin found her mind wandering away from the film at times, as she looked around the room at the absorbed faces turned to the flickering screen. She felt a warm sense of wellbeing, snuggled up in the midst of this large friendly bickering family. Yet she could also feel the subtle, invisible constraints and expectations that hung around Rukhsana. She could see how the tension between Rukhsana's love and her impatience with her parents sometimes broke out in a sharp word or gesture. Yasmin stared at the screen, unseeing, and thought about Maggie, who never seemed to expect anything of Yasmin except that she be sensible and happy. She felt deeply appreciative of their relaxed relationship, yet she had begun to realise that their perceptions of happiness differed and there were real tensions between them. Sitting in Rukhsana's comfortable, elegant shalwar kameez, curled up in an old armchair in the back room, with Nasrin on the floor in front of her leaning against her knees, Yasmin felt a kind of contentment she couldn't imagine describing to Maggie. She felt she had discovered a new richness in her life, precious but fragile, which she was not sure could withstand exposure to others' critical gaze. She felt she needed more time to nurture the new feelings about herself that were unfolding inside her, but she was also very excited about these changes. Most of all, she felt a great tenderness towards Rukhsana for changing everything, but so unobtrusively that it felt as natural as the gentle slide from autumn into winter in the trees outside her window.

The film ended happily, with all the characters in floods of emotional tears. As she followed Rukhsana up to bed, Yasmin felt a warm tired satisfaction.

10

CROSSED WIRES

Yasmin wore Rukhsana's shalwar kameez all day Saturday as well and dared to go out in it to the local shops with Rukhsana and Shaheen. They visited some sari centres, looking for material for a new suit for Rukhsana. After much persuasion, Yasmin chose some dark red material for herself, which Shaheen promised to sew for her before her next visit. They also did some food shopping in the bustling open market and returned the previous night's film to a small Asian video shop, where Yasmin felt very self-conscious under the curious gaze of the young man behind the counter. The weekend passed quickly, yet by the time they left to get the coach back late on Sunday afternoon, Yasmin felt she knew each member of the family really well, even the taciturn Shabir, and she felt quite sorry to have to leave so soon.

Both she and Rukhsana had a lot of work to catch up on when they returned to college and they scarcely saw each other on Monday. On Tuesday morning Yasmin was leaving for lectures when she saw Rukhsana emerge from her room in her dressing gown.

"Morning, you're up early!" she smiled, looking up as she locked her door.

"Mmm..." Rukhsana murmured, walking past Yasmin without looking at her.

"Are you okay?" Yasmin was a little surprised.

Rukhsana turned round abruptly and said, "Actually no, I'm not okay, but does it matter? You don't need to worry about me, do you?"

"Rukhsana, what ARE you talking about?" Yasmin asked looking at her hard set face in astonishment, she looked drained and her eyes were tired and red.

"I think you know," Rukhsana replied coldly. "How

could you come home with me and spend all weekend like that, in my own home, and not say anything? Oh, but I forgot, you're very good at keeping things to yourself, aren't you?"

"I don't know what you're talking about," Yasmin wailed in dismay.

"Ask Vikram," Rukhsana snapped. "And you can forget that meal with him and Sajid tonight." She wheeled round again and walked off down the corridor.

"Rukhsana, please!" Yasmin called after her but Rukhsana had already disappeared into the bathroom, sliding the door heavily behind her.

Yasmin waited a few minutes and then unlocked her door again and went back into her room. She would be late for her seminar but she didn't really care, she was too shaken to go out anywhere. She threw her jacket and rucksack on the bed and slumped in the armchair, staring miserably at the scuff marks on the cork tiles.

`What did she mean, "ask Vikram"?' she thought. `Is this something to do with when I saw him in the bar that time, when I was with Ben? I never told her about that, it didn't seem very important at the time. Surely she doesn't have a problem with Ben as well? I don't believe it. Or is it about last week, when Vikram bought me that coffee in the snack bar and grabbed my hand?'

She had been trying, with moderate success, to forget the incident, since she had first thought about it at Rukhsana's and decided not to say anything. At that time it had seemed much better forgotten but now she wished she had thought a bit more before deciding to keep quiet. She wondered uneasily what Vikram had been saying.

The bathroom door slid open and Yasmin heard footsteps padding back up the corridor. She listened as Rukhsana went back into her room and wondered if she should go across and try to talk to her. She felt racked with indecision and frightened of making things worse but she needed to know why Rukhsana was so angry. She sat paralysed for many long agonising minutes, until she heard Rukhsana emerge, close her door and turn the key in the lock, her bangles chinking gently on her wrist. Panicking suddenly as she realised she was letting an opportunity slip by, Yasmin leapt out of her seat and rushed to the door.

"Rukhsana!" she called after the figure hurrying away towards the double doors.

"I'm in a hurry," Rukhsana called back scarcely looking round, and she pushed through the doors, leaving them swinging loudly behind her.

Yasmin closed her own door and leant back against it, baffled. This time she knew that somehow she had really messed it up. She tried to remember every word of every conversation she had ever had with Vikram. What had she said wrong? Or what had he told Rukhsana? Maybe he wasn't supposed to be in the bar that night when she had been there with Ben, could he have lied to explain why he was there? Or maybe he had told some lie about them having coffee together, but then why mention it in the first place, when he had asked Yasmin not to say anything? Yasmin wished desperately that she had told Rukhsana about both these incidents, she felt a heavy hopelessness at the prospect of trying to convince her that she had not meant to hide anything. But then it could be something else, something she had no idea about as yet, it was all so confusing.

She walked over to her desk and sat down, tearing a sheet of blank paper from a writing pad she kept there. She picked a biro out of the red cylindrical desk tidy and began writing.

`Dear Rukhsana,
        I'm really upset that you're so angry with me. I don't understand what I've done, I never meant to upset you. If this is all about having coffee with Vikram in the snack bar the other day, or about when he was in the bar.'

She stopped as she remembered she didn't know for sure if it was either of these. If it was something else, like the dinner tonight that had been cancelled, for instance, she could just be making things worse. She screwed up the piece of paper and, taking another, began again.

`Dear Rukhsana,
        I'm really sorry you're so upset. I never intended to hurt you and I don't really know what I've done. Please can we talk about it, I think there may have been some misunderstanding. I couldn't bear it if we weren't friends.
                    Love,
                        Yasmin.'

She folded it carefully and wrote Rukhsana's name on the outside. Then, gathering up her things from the bed, she left the room, locking the door behind her for the second time that morning, and slipped the note gently under Rukhsana's door.

The next few days went painfully slowly for Yasmin. Rukhsana did not come back to hall that night or the next, and Yasmin decided to stay away from the Asian Society meeting, not wanting to meet her in a crowd of people. She filled her days with seminars and lectures and all the outstanding tasks she had allowed to pile up, like writing to old penfriends and getting her jacket dry-cleaned. She avoided getting into long conversations with most people, pretending to be very busy, and stayed in at night, working furiously to escape her thoughts and only going to bed when she was so exhausted she could scarcely lift her drooping eyelids to peer at the blurred page. Even then, sleep did not come easily as she rehearsed endless speeches to Rukhsana in her head, explaining what had happened and why she had kept quiet.

On Wednesday afternoon she bumped into Sharon and Fiona on their way to have tea at a cafe near the university, and she joined them reluctantly. They sat at the front of the cafe by the window, which had steamed over and was littered with small cards and notices sellotaped to the glass, periodically attracting the absorbed attention of passers-by.

"Why don't you come? You're not doing anything this weekend, are you?" Sharon asked Yasmin, having just described a party she and Fiona were invited to that Friday night.

"I don't know yet," Yasmin replied evasively. "I might even go home, I haven't decided."

"I thought you'd just been," Fiona interrupted. "Is everything all right?"

"Fine. It's nearly four weeks since I went, actually, you must be thinking of last weekend when I went to Rukhsana's."

"Probably," Fiona murmured unconvinced. "But you do go home a lot. I haven't been back all term, you miss all the fun going away at the weekend."

"Was it all right at Rukhsana's, then?" Sharon asked curiously.

"Yeah, it was great, her family are really nice," Yasmin said enthusiastically, realising that she couldn't tell them anything about what had happened since, she would feel too disloyal. She could imagine how Trish would gloat, hearing of a split between Rukhsana and herself.

"Yaz is having Rukhsana to stay in the holidays as well," Sharon informed Fiona. "They're really into visiting each other's families."

"Oh God! I wouldn't let my parents near my friends, or vice versa!" Fiona exclaimed. "Your mother must be something else."

"She's okay," Yasmin smiled faintly. "Anyway, it's not definite yet, Rukhsana might have to stay here to work."

"It was interesting that stuff we were doing with Miss Mellor yesterday, wasn't it?" Sharon said thoughtfully. "You know, the Indo-European language family and all that? Does Rukhsana speak Hindi?"

"Urdu. Well, she mainly speaks Punjabi at home, but her Mum taught her Urdu as well and she did it for `O' level in school."

"Do they have `O' levels in Pakistan?" Fiona interrupted.

"Not Pakistan, she did it in London. You can do it in lots of schools."

"It's funny to think of our languages being related," Sharon mused. "They sound so different, Hindi and those other Indian languages, but they're probably closer to English than Welsh is. What does your Dad speak, Yasmin?"

"Same as Rukhsana, Punjabi and Urdu," Yasmin replied confidently. "Actually, it made me think about learning Urdu properly."

"Haven't you had enough doing French all day?" Fiona teased. "You'd just get confused."

"That's not true," Sharon argued. "It's supposed to be that the more languages you learn the better you are at picking up new ones, your brain gets quicker at adjusting or something, it was in a book on language acquisition I looked through for that last essay."

"Maybe you should start learning Urdu and we'll do a study on how you learn," Fiona suggested eagerly. "Do you think you'd learn it faster than us? It might be buried in your brain somewhere from hearing it when you were little."

"I don't think so," Yasmin laughed awkwardly. "I think my Dad spoke English to us. Anyway, I haven't got time to learn a whole new language."

"Oh go on, I think it would make a really good project," Fiona insisted fired up with the idea. "We could do it as a joint paper, the three of us, and present it to the linguistics seminar instead of doing individual ones. Say you'll think about it."

"Maybe," Yasmin stalled wondering what Rukhsana would think of her learning Urdu as a linguistics experiment.

"Are you coming down to the Kings' Arms tonight?"

Fiona asked, changing tack as she saw that Yasmin was not to be pushed on the subject of Urdu.

"Yasmin always goes to her Asian Club on Wednesdays, and we wouldn't want to interfere with that," Sharon said with an edge of sarcasm.

"Oh fuck off, Sharon!" Yasmin flared, suddenly.

Sharon and Fiona stared at her, shocked. She stood up abruptly, her chair grating loudly across the floor, and hurried out of the cafe. She felt more lonely now than she had done before she bumped into Sharon and Fiona. She made her way home through the darkening streets, longing for the kindly solitude of her own room, despite the painful silence across the corridor.

The next evening she went out to the youth club, relieved to be able to absorb herself in another world for a while and be carried on the tide of the children's easy joys and excitements. She was pleased to see Ben, and they spent the second half of the evening in the union bar with Maureen and Hilary, talking about safe, general things. It was not until the two of them were waiting at the bus stop for the bus back to their halls that she got a chance to speak to him alone.

"So what's the matter with you tonight?" he began, his breath coming out in small steamy clouds that evaporated into the frosty air. "You've hardly said a word all night."

"Oh, everything," Yasmin muttered gloomily. "I've upset Rukhsana and she's not speaking to me, it's a real mess and I feel awful."

"Oh dear, what have you done?"

"Well, that's just it. I don't really know. Do you remember her boyfriend, Vikram? I met him at the bar that night, the night you told me you were gay."

"Oh yeah."

"Well, when I asked her what was wrong she said, `ask Vikram'. I met him again last week and he dragged me off for a drink in the snack bar and started going on at me about what an unsuitable partner you were."

Ben burst out laughing.

"I know," Yasmin smiled. "He made a right fool of himself, if only he'd known, but he asked me not to tell Rukhsana in case she was cross with him for interfering, or something. Anyway, I said okay because it didn't seem very important and I was a bit embarrassed about the whole thing, so I didn't want to tell her myself."

"Why embarrassed?"

"Oh, he was really slimy and he grabbed my hand, it was horrible. I didn't want to tell Rukhsana that."

"Maybe she should know," Ben muttered grimly.

"Maybe, but it wouldn't help now, because she's probably upset I never said anything before. I never told her about seeing him in the bar that night either."

"So, how might she have found out about these secret rendezvous?" Ben asked with the suggestion of a twinkle in his eye.

"It's not funny."

"I'm sorry."

"He must have told her, I suppose, after he'd asked me not to say anything, stupid idiot. So now it looks like I was trying to hide something."

"But why would he tell her? Wouldn't he get into trouble too?"

"Oh, I don't know," Yasmin sighed. "Maybe it just came out by accident. Or maybe it's not that anyway, it might be something Vikram's heard about me, or something else that connects him and me that I don't even know about and she thinks I do. It doesn't really matter, all that matters is that she won't speak to me and that makes me really sad."

"Well, she's not much of a mate if she'll listen to him and not you," Ben said angrily. "She sounds a bit of a drama queen to me, I don't see what's so horrendous about you having coffee with Vikram or bumping into him in a bar."

"No, it's not like her," Yasmin admitted. "I think it's to do with me not saying anything. You see, it happened once before, she got upset when she found out I hadn't

127

told my other friends about her, she said I was ashamed of her, though she knew it was rubbish. It feels like it's all connected."

"Well she expects too much if she thinks she has to be told everything all the time, are you sure she's worth being friends with?"

"Oh yes," Yasmin replied earnestly. "I don't understand what's happening, but I'm sure if we could talk she would know I haven't done anything to hurt her."

"Sounds to me like she's running away from you," Ben suggested. "It's all very convenient putting it onto some two-minute meeting with Vikram. Why won't she talk to you herself?"

"I don't know. She's being so mysterious and I miss her like anything. It's so boring without her..."

"Thanks!"

"Oh, you know what I mean. I can't concentrate on anything, I just think about it all the time."

"You better watch yourself, you sound seriously hooked!" Ben teased.

"What do you mean?"

"Nothing," Ben shrugged. "So then, what are you going to do about it?"

"I can't do anything if she won't talk to me."

"That's the answer then," Ben said firmly. "You know what you want, you've just really got to go for it, man. You've got to make her sit down and listen to you and if she doesn't stop her nonsense after that, you send her to me!"

Yasmin laughed at his vehemence and looked up as the bus appeared at the top of the road, its headlights cutting through the dense freezing fog. They found seats at the back and continued talking in low voices.

"So you didn't go to your meeting last night, then?" Ben concluded quietly.

"No, I couldn't, they're all Rukhsana's friends and Vikram might have been there as well, it would have been really awkward for all of us."

"But what about all your stuff about your father and being Asian and everything, you were just getting into feeling good about it all?"

"I don't know, I feel like Rukhsana's my only link."

"Apart from your Mum."

"Yes, but she doesn't really understand what it's like for me now, she just thinks about the past and then she panics about me thinking about the past and, anyway -" Yasmin stopped suddenly.

"And anyway, she's white and you're not?" Ben suggested.

"Something like that," Yasmin replied slowly, wondering what her mother really thought about it all. Then she changed the subject quickly saying, "Anyway, how are you getting on?"

"Oh, brilliant!" Ben beamed apologetically. "I won't bore you with the details, but it's great not to feel so alone and I'm meeting loads of new people, thanks to you pushing me."

"Yes, but you did it," Yasmin insisted, "I think it's great, you seem much happier already. Are you going to tell your parents now?"

"You must be joking!" Ben mocked. "I might start with my sister, I think I could cope with that, then I'll see what she thinks about telling The Parents!"

"Don't you think your Mum knows?"

"Why should she?"

"My Mum knows everything about me, that's why I haven't phoned again this week, she'd know straight away I'm upset about something. Trouble is, she knows when I don't ring as well!"

"Maybe you're right," Ben assented. "But if my mother has any ideas about me she keeps them to herself. I think she just hopes I'll get a girlfriend and it'll all go away."

The bus reached their stop and they got off and walked back to their halls in contemplative silence, lost in their own thoughts. A thick white frost lay on the grass and paths, and the bitter cold seeped through their clothes slowly extinguishing the warm glow lingering from the stuffy over-heated bus.

"I think I'll definitely go home this weekend," Yasmin announced suddenly as they reached the entrance to her hall. "I can't bear a whole weekend here like this."

"Well you can always come over and see me," Ben offered.

"Thanks."

"Except Saturday night. I may be going out with a new friend," he winked mysteriously.

"Don't worry, I think I need to go home, there are some things I want to sort out with Mum and I can't talk to her properly on the phone."

"Suit yourself," Ben shrugged easily. "Pop round anytime you feel like talking. I'm off now, it's freezing! See you!" and he ran off into the gloom.

The next morning Yasmin woke early still thinking about her conversation with Ben and his advice to go and have it out with Rukhsana. She knew where Rukhsana would be and decided she would go over to Shahnaz and Atiya's first thing and catch Rukhsana before she went out.

The house was in an old terraced back street not far from the city centre. When Yasmin arrived the curtains were still drawn tight in the front room downstairs, but there were lights on in some of the bedrooms and the kitchen. She went round to the back door and knocked loudly before she could lose her nerve. There was a long silence and then, through the window, she saw Atiya hurrying through the dining room into the kitchen to open the door. She was still pulling on a sweater over her crumpled shirt as she opened the door. When she saw Yasmin her face hardened angrily.

"What the hell do you think you're doing coming round here at this hour?" she said roughly.

"I'd like to see Rukhsana," Yasmin said in what she hoped was a quiet, firm voice.

"She's not here, she went to get the bus ten minutes

ago," Atiya replied shortly, looking Yasmin up and down with disgust.

"Are you sure? I didn't see her on the main road."

"Of course I'm sure. Anyway, I don't think she'd want to see you if she was here, after what you've done."

"But that's what I came to talk about, I don't know what I'm supposed to have done," Yasmin persisted urgently.

"And you've got the cheek to say that to my face!" Atiya exclaimed incredulously. "God, you've got a nerve."

"Can I come in and talk about this?" Yasmin suggested. "Or we'll both freeze with the door open like that."

"Oh please yourself, just walk right in," Atiya invited sarcastically, holding the door open in an exaggerated gesture.

Yasmin walked in calmly, feeling slightly sick in her stomach, but determined to find out what was going on. She leaned against the kitchen door frame without taking her coat off, while Atiya filled a kettle and put some bread in the toaster.

"So come on then, what do you want to say? Because I've got to have some breakfast and get to college before ten o'clock," Atiya challenged with evident irritation.

"I just want to know what people have been saying about me. I mean, what's Vikram been saying because it's got to be lies to cause this much trouble?"

"He's saying as little as possible, I think, he knows he's made a mess of it. But I don't blame him, I blame you, he's just too stupid to see through your scheming."

"What scheming?" Yasmin cried in frustration, "I don't know what you're talking about!"

"Oh yes! Go on, act the little innocent first year! Well, you may be able to fool Rukhsana, but I can see right through you, madam," Atiya spat out her words venomously. "Ever since you came you've tried to muscle in on every part of Rukhsana's life, cosy little dinners, midnight feasts, angling your way into the

131

Asian Soc., even inviting yourself to her parents' house!...And now you've ruined her lovely romance for her, well I hope you're pleased with yourself."

"I'm sorry if something's gone wrong between her and Vikram," Yasmin said carefully, gripping the door frame to give herself strength against Atiya's tirades. "But it can't be anything to do with me, I hardly know Vikram."

"Are you serious?" Atiya scoffed, pausing as she poured her tea out to stare at Yasmin in baffled amazement.

"Yes, and all that about me taking over Rukhsana's life is rubbish too, she invited me to meet her family, and to the Asian Soc. I don't want to muscle in on anything."

"Well you have," Atiya stated emphatically. "We were quite happy, all of us, 'till you came on the scene. I don't know how you managed to get your claws into Rukhsana. She wouldn't talk about anyone else. It was Yasmin this, and Yasmin that, and let's all look after Yasmin because she's a poor little first year who doesn't know who she is!" She swept past Yasmin into the dining room and sat down at the table with her tea and toast, ignoring Yasmin still standing by the door.

"Rukhsana isn't sorry for me, she likes me," Yasmin asserted moving over to the table and sitting down opposite Atiya.

"Well you can't get out of the stuff about Vikram because I saw you in that coffee bar," Atiya smiled triumphantly. "So let's see how you explain that."

Yasmin suddenly remembered, with dawning understanding, bumping into Atiya as she went out of the coffee bar that day. Atiya had said she hadn't been in yet, but she must have been inside already and seen Yasmin and Vikram, when she so innocently asked Yasmin if she had seen Shahnaz. Yasmin felt momentarily floored at this realisation, she supposed it did look bad now, the fact that she hadn't told Rukhsana about it.

"But what's so awful about having coffee in a public

place?" she responded, rallying her arguments. "I am allowed to talk to Vikram, I suppose?"

"You were doing more than just talking," Atiya snorted, contemptuously. "You were all over each other, I saw you, holding hands and kissing and looking deeply into each other's eyes, it was sickening."

"Kissing?" Yasmin shrieked in disbelief. "You couldn't have! You're not saying you actually saw us kiss, surely?"

"More or less, I didn't have the best view, it's true, but there was enough else going on to know what you were up to."

Yasmin was silent as she digested this new information. She felt no desire to justify herself to Atiya, but she could see now why Rukhsana was so upset and she knew she had to make her see the truth.

"You don't know what you're talking about," she said finally. "It's very dangerous to repeat things you don't understand. Why didn't you ask me about it at the time?"

"I didn't think you'd want to discuss it, given the circumstances," Atiya replied smugly. "And you seemed in a bit of a rush."

"Well you've got it wrong, but I can't be bothered explaining because you won't believe me whatever I say. When will Rukhsana be back tonight?"

"She won't, she's going home to her parents after lectures this afternoon, she's taken her bag with her. You can ask Shahnaz if you can be bothered waiting for her to get up."

"No, it's all right, I'm going home too," Yasmin sighed getting up to leave. "Thanks for the explanation, you really have got it all wrong. I wouldn't kiss Vikram if you paid me, he's a creep. But you don't have to believe me."

"Don't worry, I don't," Atiya smiled humourlessly, and she let Yasmin out, slamming the door behind her.

Yasmin trailed dispiritedly back through the cold wintry streets to the bus stop on the main road. She felt shaken by the encounter, and the violence of Atiya's feelings, but relieved that she at least understood what had gone wrong. She thought back over what Atiya had said and felt quite comforted to know how much she mattered to Rukhsana. 'Surely she wouldn't just turn her back on me without even thinking about it?' she thought. As she went over the things Atiya had said, a slow amazement stirred inside her. 'Atiya said she wouldn't talk about anyone else. I didn't know she even thought about me when we weren't together, she's got so many other friends.' She smiled, amused, and hugged herself as a little shiver of crazy optimism ran through her.

11

HOME RETREAT

Yasmin and Maggie sat by the fire in the front room, watching television in an atmosphere of quiet waiting. The room was lit by a tall standard lamp behind Maggie's chair, which shed a soft golden light from behind its pale shade. Maggie was knitting methodically, looking alternately at the television screen and the pattern lying open on the arm of her chair, her fingers following the familiar manipulations with practised ease. Occasionally she passed a comment, some innocuous question about Yasmin's work, or a snippet of local news. Yasmin lay curled up on the deep, high-backed settee, leaning against a cushion at one end, with her legs tucked up beside her and one arm folded behind her head. Her old red jumper sagged shapelessly and its loose stretched sleeves gaped open, letting cool air in to chill her bare forearms. She stared fixedly at the television, but she was not listening to the dialogue and her mind raced over the complications and confusions of the last few weeks.

"Mum?" she said at length.

"Mmm..." Maggie murmured calmly, squinting at her pattern to check which stitch came next.

"When you're telling people about me, what do you say?"

"I say you're my daughter, what do you mean?" Maggie replied looking up at her sharply.

"But what if they ask about my name?"

"I tell them who your Dad was, and I suppose sometimes I might say we chose your name together, it depends on the conversation."

"But you don't say I'm mixed race?"

"No, not usually, I don't like general terms like that, you're an individual and you've got a name, what more do you need?" Maggie explained slowly as if feeling her way. "I don't call myself anything, not English or Irish, or anything else, so why should I put a label on you?"

"But people don't ask about you," Yasmin argued struggling to find the words she needed. "They're always asking about me, they can see I'm not English."

"But once you've explained about your father, surely that's an end of it?" Maggie said anxiously, pausing in the middle of her stitch to scrutinise Yasmin's face. "Has someone been having a go at you, love?"

"No, it's not that," Yasmin reassured her. "It's just that I feel there's more to it than simply explaining that my Dad was Asian. I feel different, but I don't know what to call myself."

"But you never said you felt different before," Maggie insisted. "All through school weren't you just the same as all the other girls? If someone's making you feel different now, then they're wrong. We're all basically the same underneath, I've always believed that."

"But weren't you different from my Dad?" Yasmin asked, thinking that people didn't get treated the same, even if they were the same, which she very much doubted.

"We were different people, but it wasn't because he was Asian and I was British, it was just because we were two different individuals. And we understood each other, we had the same feelings about a lot of things."

Yasmin fell silent, trying to identify why she felt her mother was wrong, even though her words sounded so rational. She felt nervous about pursuing the subject, but she desperately wanted to sort out for herself why what you called yourself mattered. She looked sideways at Maggie, who was staring down intently through her twisting fingers and flashing needles to some imagined place beyond. Yasmin wondered if she was scared too and felt suddenly protective of her.

"Is this why you came home?" Maggie asked eventually, looking up from her work.

"Sort of, I've had such a lot to think about lately, I

wanted a break and I wanted to ask you some things."

"Like why I don't call you mixed race?"

"Yeah," Yasmin paused, and then continued speculatively. "How do you think my Dad would have described me to other people?"

"For goodness' sake, Yasmin!" Maggie laughed loudly, putting her knitting down in her lap. "I don't think I should have encouraged you to go to university if this is the kind of question you come back with! I've no idea what he would have said. But you would have been different anyway if he'd stuck around, we'd all have been different, I expect."

"How do you mean?"

"Well, like when you went to school, you might have kept your original name."

"Yasmin Siddique? Like on my birth certificate?"

"Yes, though that was only a mistake really, because they thought we were married and your father had a sudden fit of coyness and was too embarrassed to say otherwise. We weren't very organised about registering your name, as I remember. But by the time you got to school it was much easier for you to have the same name as me. Does that worry you now?"

"Oh no, I'm quite happy with my name as it is," Yasmin assured her. "I'm just interested to think what I would have been like if I'd grown up more Asian."

"But you were never interested in anything Asian before," Maggie insisted defensively. "Is Rukhsana making you feel bad because you're not a Muslim?"

"No, no!" Yasmin laughed. "It's not about being a Muslim. In fact, since I've met Rukhsana I've been feeling miles better about all these things."

"You never said you felt bad before," Maggie interrupted again dismayed. "Why didn't you tell me?"

"I don't mean I felt bad," Yasmin denied hastily. "I hardly thought about it before, but I suppose I must have known there was something there waiting to be thought about whenever I got round to it. Now I've met Rukhsana I've started doing that thinking, that's all."

"But she's making you feel different, that worries me," Maggie said looking dubious. "I feel like she's trying to change you."

"She's not doing anything, it's me," Yasmin stressed earnestly. "I'm changing myself. I suppose if I hadn't met her it might have taken longer, but I'd still end up asking all these questions sometime, wouldn't I?" Maggie did not reply, she took up her knitting again and seemed lost in thought over what had been said.

Yasmin got up and went into the kitchen to put the kettle on, wondering whether she should let it all drop or try harder to explain how she felt. She hardly knew herself what she was trying to explain and she wished she had been able to ask Rukhsana about it all first. She knew there were lots of things that Rukhsana wouldn't necessarily understand either, but when she was with Rukhsana it all seemed clearer somehow. She left the kettle to boil and returned to the other room. Maggie smiled warmly at her as she sat tentatively on the edge of the settee.

"I'm not criticising your friends, love, I just don't like to think that you're not happy, or that you're worrying about something," she said to Yasmin.

"I know, but I'm not worrying, I'm not miserable," Yasmin insisted, mentally discounting her present difficulty with Rukhsana as having nothing to do with what they were talking about here. "I don't know how to describe it, but being with Rukhsana and her friends makes me feel really safe and happy and comfortable. I didn't tell you because I knew you wouldn't like it, but I've been going to the Asian Students' Society with them and it's been really good, I feel right being there and there are other people like me, you know, from mixed backgrounds, so I don't feel so odd."

"I don't know," Maggie sighed with an edge of bitterness. "It sounds like I've been doing the wrong thing all these years. Maybe I should have tried to find out about your Dad's culture and teach you. I just didn't feel it had anything to do with us once he'd walked out,

I thought I was doing the best for you."

"I know you were," Yasmin interrupted fervently. "Anyway, I was too busy having a good time with my friends. Even if you'd suggested it, I might not have wanted to talk about it, it didn't mean anything to me then, honestly."

"So if you were happy, then I don't understand what the problem is," Maggie argued almost irritably.

"Maybe things about Pakistan didn't mean anything to me because all my friends were English," Yasmin suggested cautiously, thinking back to her early school days. "If we'd stayed in London or moved to a different part of Sheffield, I might have made some Asian friends when I was younger."

"And you might not," Maggie retorted, remembering all her old anxieties about sending her daughter out into the world. "I'm afraid they might not have accepted you because you're not a Muslim and because of me, and that would have been even worse."

"Rukhsana accepts me and so do plenty of other Asian people. They don't care whether I'm a Muslim or not, and anyway there are loads of different religions in Asia."

"So are you saying I shouldn't have left London?" Maggie broke in.

"No! I'm not saying you should or shouldn't have done anything!" Yasmin insisted, feeling she was being led into arguing about the wrong things. "I was happy anyway. You tell me not to worry about the past, now don't you start!"

"Okay," Maggie agreed grudgingly. "Go and make that tea, love, I could do with a cup with all this talking." She was feeling very shaky and churned up. It was like going back twelve years to when Yasmin first started school. She had worried so much then about how she would be treated and whether she would fit in. She had even considered changing her name, but the thought had felt like a betrayal of all the good feelings that had attached to naming her Yasmin in the first place. Maggie had felt she could not do it, despite Farooq's betrayal of those good times, and, besides, it would have been too disruptive for Yasmin. As she had settled down in school and made friends easily, Maggie's fears had faded and eventually she had come to feel that Yasmin was treated no different from anyone else. If she was she never said anything about it.

It was many years since Maggie had thought very much about all this and she would never have guessed that it would all flare up again when Yasmin went to university. Now she found herself once again wishing guiltily that Yasmin looked more like her, that she was lighter-skinned, then maybe she wouldn't feel the need to fret about all this so much. It worried her to think of Yasmin wanting to be with Asian girls all the time, she was bound to come up against much more prejudice and she might lose the white friends that she'd got, like that Sharon. `She hardly ever mentions her now,' Maggie thought. She had no doubt that Rukhsana and her friends were nice girls. Well, she did have her doubts about Rukhsana because of the hold she seemed to have over Yasmin. She felt that Yasmin did not see the implications of getting too involved and would get hurt in the end. Maggie had such an uneasy feeling about it all.

Yasmin made the tea and fetched a cake tin from the old cupboard built into the kitchen wall. They settled down again with tea and fruit cake to an episode of Maggie's favourite detective series, which they watched in a slightly tense, self-conscious silence. Yasmin could not concentrate on the programme and found herself feeling irritated with her mother for seeing everything in such a negative light. Why did Maggie always think she was criticising her for the way she was brought up? She realised she had expected it to be like this, that was why she had been putting it off all term. But she wished Maggie could understand the revolution that had taken place in her life these last few weeks, she wanted her acceptance and approval, not all these fears and suspicions and doubts about the past.

She wished she had someone to talk to who really understood exactly what all this felt like, a sister or brother who had grown up in the same circumstances and would understand without taking it all so personally. She remembered the strange feeling when she first saw Nasrin, looking like a younger reflection of Rukhsana in her yellow shalwar kameez, and thought how different it must be to grow up surrounded by a host of older and younger reflections of yourself. She thought about the first time she went to Rukhsana's room and how good she had felt, what a revelation it had been to spend time with someone who linked in with the side of herself she knew nothing about. She remembered how excited and relieved she had been at the Diwali party when she realised it was okay for her to be there and the warm feeling of acceptance she felt at her first Asian Soc. meeting. She wanted her mother to understand what it was about these experiences that was so important. But she realised she could not say herself.

`Maybe I'm chasing after something that's just an illusion,' she thought, `but it felt like I was starting to get to grips with it all when I met Rukhsana, and where is she now?' Yasmin suddenly felt a surge of anger at the thought of her isolation from Rukhsana. `She starts me off on all this and then she just dumps me,' she thought, `she knows how difficult it all is for me. I can't just go and see Shahnaz or Manjula on my own and I can't go to the Asian Soc. when she's not speaking to me, it's like it's her territory and I was just a guest, but now I'm not welcome any more. But that's not fair, I do have a right to go too, otherwise what's all this been about? Either I'm Asian or I'm not, and if I am then I can be Asian without Rukhsana, can't I ?'

The power of this idea seized Yasmin so forcibly she almost leapt out of her seat. She turned it over in her mind, and wondered if she really dared go to the Asian Society meeting alone, just as herself, rather than as

Rukhsana's friend. But it wasn't just a question of going because she had a right to, it was a question of whether she could stand the strain and tension of being in the same room as Rukhsana for two hours without speaking to her. Yasmin realised she could not imagine putting herself or Rukhsana through that. She remembered Rukhsana's pained and exhausted face disappearing through the double doors on the corridor. `This silly misunderstanding is hurting Rukhsana too,' she thought, sadly.

"Have you asked Rukhsana what she'd like to do when she comes up ?" Maggie asked, her voice breaking into Yasmin's thoughts.

"Not yet, we've been really busy," Yasmin stalled, thinking fast. "She's got so much work on at the moment, I hope she'll be able to come."

"She can always bring some of it with her, " Maggie smiled reassuringly. "We won't mind if she spends an hour or two at your old desk upstairs, if it makes her feel better."

"Well, let's see," Yasmin cautioned. "I could invite her another time if this holiday seems a bad idea."

"Surely the next one will be much worse ? She'll be busy revising for finals and you'll have your first year exams to worry about. No, I think she'll have to come this vacation if she's coming," Maggie said definitely.

Yasmin decided it was safer to change the subject. "I thought I might pop round to see Jenny tomorrow morning," she said. "She doesn't know I'm here, but I could surprise her and we could go out for a drink or a walk or something."

"That'd be nice," Maggie agreed, "I'm sure she misses you, I bump into her sometimes at Safeways and she always asks when you're coming home and what you're doing with yourself."

"I've been writing to her. It's just a bit difficult now we're doing such different things."

"I'm sure you can describe it all beautifully, you're very good with words and we all love to read about what you're doing," Maggie insisted.

"Okay, point taken," Yasmin conceded. They both looked up, startled, as the door swung quietly open and the cat, Tibby, padded in serenely and jumped onto the settee. Yasmin settled her gently on her lap while Maggie continued to knit, thinking about Yasmin's beautiful descriptive letters.

"Your father's a fool," she muttered suddenly, flicking her needles angrily. "He doesn't know what he's missed not seeing you growing up into such a lovely young woman. I don't know why we waste our breath even talking about him, he doesn't deserve a second of our time, leaving behind a beautiful, intelligent, talented daughter like you to fret and worry about where she's come from."

"But we weren't talking about him," Yasmin argued, taken aback by her mother's anger.

"Well that's what this is really all about, isn't it ?" Maggie said grimly. "If he'd stayed with us you'd have his name and you'd know all about Pakistan and you'd be happy. I can't tell you about all that, can I? So you had to wait 'till you meet some stranger at university to find out what you wanted to know," her voice quivered and broke and she shut her mouth firmly as her eyes began to water.

"Oh, Mum, don't get upset!" Yasmin cried rushing over to her and putting her arms around her shoulders. "I don't care about him, or whether he was here or not, it's his loss, isn't it ?"

Maggie nodded sniffing, and fumbled in her sleeve for a tissue.

"It's not about him, it's about me," Yasmin continued passionately. "I'm just trying to find out what to call myself, who I am, you know."

"But I don't understand why you have to call yourself anything," Maggie said looking perplexed, her eyes were red and watery and Yasmin noticed how wrinkled they were at the corners, and how many grey hairs there were curled around her temples.

"Well, not call myself, exactly," she qualified, "more where I place myself in relation to everyone else, do you know what I mean ?"

"I don't know if I do," Maggie sighed. "I just don't agree with all this labelling and categorising. Life's more complicated than a few blanket terms, isn't it? I think making categories just encourages conflict."

"But what if the conflict's already there?" Yasmin suggested, remembering some of the discussions between Rukhsana and the others about racism, and thinking of her experiences at school with John Griffiths and the geography teacher who stood by and let it happen. "Then you have to decide where you stand."

"So somebody has been getting at you," Maggie concluded triumphantly, "I knew it."

"Oh Mum!" Yasmin drew back in exasperation and sat heavily on the floor at Maggie's feet. "You just don't understand. All I'm saying is I feel like I want to call myself Asian, or at least mixed race Asian. That's all I'm saying."

"But you're not really Asian are you, love," Maggie coaxed softly. "You've grown up so English, it's too late to start pretending now, you're as English as Jenny or me in everything except your name."

"And the colour of my skin, and my hair," Yasmin added pointedly. "People don't see me as English, you know they don't."

"But you can't deny what you are just because other people say you're something else, they're just ignorant and prejudiced if they think you're not English. They haven't caught up with the fact that there are whole generations of people like you in this country who have grown up here and have every right to call themselves English."

"Okay Mum, I agree with all that, I guess. I'm a British citizen but I'm not English in the same way as you, I mean I'm not white, am I? I don't feel very English either, I've always felt a bit different, like I'm something else, and going to things like the Asian Society feels like it's helping me understand what that something else might be."

"So you want to be like your Dad rather than me?" Maggie cried emotionally. "You'd rather call yourself Asian when he deserted you without a second thought and hasn't shown a flicker of interest in you for the last fifteen years? Is that really what you want?"

"I told you it's nothing to do with him," Yasmin insisted desperately. "It's what I want!"

Suddenly they heard the back door slam and they both froze for a moment. Then Yasmin slid back across to the settee as the television babbled on and Maggie picked up her knitting. Rod opened the door and grinned broadly at both of them.

"Hello, you two look cosy in here, what are you watching?"

"Oh, some rubbish, we were talking," Maggie replied looking at Yasmin conspiratorially.

"Do you want a drink, Rod, I was just going to make some coffee?" Yasmin offered, getting up from her seat.

Rod nodded agreement and took Yasmin's place on the settee, looking searchingly at Maggie.

"Everything okay?" he asked when Yasmin had closed the kitchen door.

"No, but don't ask, it's my problem," Maggie replied firmly. "I don't understand what's happening to her, but if I find that friend of her's is at the bottom of all this, I shall have something to say to her when she comes up here."

"Be careful who you go blaming," Rod cautioned. "I should think Yasmin's quite capable of creating her own dramas, in fact I'll have a bone to pick with her myself if she goes upsetting you any more."

"You keep out of it," Maggie muttered sternly, as they heard the kitchen door opening again.

Yasmin returned with three cups of coffee and they all sat chatting for a while. The atmosphere of forced cheerfulness soon wore Yasmin down and she finished her drink and went up to bed, explaining that she was very tired.

Later, lying in bed, she could hear Maggie and Rod talking in the big bedroom below. Their voices were too muffled to distinguish any words, but she could hear their low, worried tones and she imagined they were talking about her. `It's all right for them,' she thought, `they've got each other to talk to, who have I got?' She tried to imagine telling Jenny about the conversation with Maggie, but she couldn't, and she realised it felt very private, like she needed to be very careful who she told because they had to be people who would understand. She supposed Maggie had told Rod all about it, she didn't want him to know, it was none of his business and he wouldn't understand anyway. She turned over boisterously and pulled the covers over her head so she couldn't hear them talking any more.

12
SETTING THE RECORD STRAIGHT

Rukhsana sat at her desk covering the front page of her rough notebook with intricate doodles, elegant swirls interlocking with circle and leaf shapes, all in smooth black ink. She knew that Yasmin would be back from her Monday classes soon and they would have to talk. She had thought about refusing ever to see her again, but over the weekend she had realised she could not go on avoiding her forever. At home Nasrin had asked about her endlessly, and her mother wanted to know when Yasmin was coming to try on the suit she was sewing for her. Back here she realised it was getting a bit ridiculous, dodging in and out of the corridor all the time to avoid her. They would have to sort it out properly and finally, so they could at least get on with their lives in peace without all this uncertainty.

Her gaze roamed idly over the cluttered assembly of postcards and lists that she had pinned to the cork notice board above her desk. Below the notice board there was a tray of letters and papers that she jokingly called her `in-tray' and in it she could see the crumpled note Yasmin had poked under her door last week, peeping out beneath a letter from Farzana. She knew exactly what it said, she had read it so many times and every time she had felt twinges of confused affection and fury at the words, "I couldn't bear it if we weren't friends." The letter gave no clue as to why Yasmin should have hurt her so much when they had been so close these last few weeks. `If she couldn't bear it, why did she do something so stupid and cruel?' Rukhsana thought in weary bewilderment. Apart from the note, there was no trace of Yasmin's presence in her room. After all, they had only met at the end of

September and it should be easy enough to forget a friendship that had only lasted a few weeks. `Life's too short to waste on people who don't give you any respect,' Rukhsana thought.

She tried to prepare what she was going to say, but could not get beyond her overwhelming disappointment that Yasmin could betray her trust after all they had been to each other this term. She stabbed her pen into the paper miserably and then got up and went over to her window. The curtains were still open and she could see the street lights on the path shining through her own reflection and the reflection of the brightly lit desk behind her. She wished this wasn't happening, she wished she had never met Yasmin or Vikram. She had been quite happy for the last two years with her friends and her course work. and her work at the Citizens Advice Bureau. Now everything seemed to have turned sour and was conspiring to depress her, even the Asian Students' Society, into which she had put so much. When she thought about going to a meeting, she got an ugly churning feeling and felt she couldn't bear to face any of them, not even Atiya. She felt completely wrecked, and strangely detached from the world around her, as if she had not slept for many nights.

`It's funny, though,' she thought. `In all this mess I've hardly noticed that Vikram's gone. After all the months and years I spent daydreaming about him, he seems to have just floated out of my mind. It's like he was never there, like he was just some stranger I brushed past in the street. It's Atiya who's in a state about us splitting up, not me. Maybe he never was there, it was just the idea of him that I loved.' She realised it was Yasmin she missed, Yasmin she still caught herself talking to in her head in unguarded moments, whose absence was like losing her own voice.

She started as she heard a door being unlocked and recognised it as Yasmin's door. Quickly, she delved in the pockets of the jacket hanging on the back of her chair and found her room key with its metal college tag. She went out, locking the door behind her, and stuffed the key into her cardigan pocket. Then she hurried across to Yasmin's room.

Yasmin opened the door as soon as she heard Rukhsana's knock. They looked at each other for a moment in a tense, uncertain silence. Rukhsana felt her stomach caving in, even as she told herself that she was in the right and should be strong. Then Yasmin said quickly, "Come in, I was just about to come across myself, actually, I'm dying to talk you."

"I know, I got your note last week," Rukhsana replied cautiously.

"Sit down, I'll make some tea," Yasmin invited.

Rukhsana watched in silence as Yasmin hurriedly made the drink, feeling almost sorry for her as she fumbled with the tightly sealed opening of a new carton of milk, Rukhsana wanted to help, but she did not want to appear to be relenting in any way. She looked at Yasmin's concentrated frown, her long brown fingers and the creamy pearl-inlaid bangles rattling on her wrist that Rukhsana had given her that weekend at home. She felt like asking for them back, but decided that would be too petty.

Once they both had a mug of tea, Yasmin sat on the chair by her desk while Rukhsana settled in the armchair opposite her, perching her mug on the flat wooden arm.

"Look, I know what you think happened," Yasmin began, "but it wasn't like that at all, there's been a stupid misunderstanding."

"That's what Vikram said," Rukhsana sighed wearily, her fingers playing on the rim of the steaming hot mug. "He gave me a pile of excuses a mile long, so I shouldn't bother thinking of any more."

"But you have to listen to the truth, Rukhsana, it's me saying it," Yasmin urged passionately. "We never kissed or anything, what was going on in that coffee bar was totally unromantic, it was horrible."

"Oh, stop it," Rukhsana snapped angrily. "Stop pretending. It's embarrassing. Atiya saw you, she told me

149

he leant right across the table and kissed you."

"And I know what I did!" Yasmin cried indignantly. "Atiya couldn't see properly. It's true Vikram did hold my hand. But I didn't want him to, he was being really slimy, telling me he'd fix me up with Sajid and he wanted to look after me, and stuff, and he just grabbed my hand. I tried to pull it away, but he held on, I didn't want it to happen, honestly, I hate him!"

"So why didn't you tell me?" Rukhsana retorted suspiciously.

"Because I was embarrassed, I suppose, and if I told you he'd been pestering me you'd have been really upset. What would you have said if I told you I thought your boyfriend was a creep? I didn't know how to tell you I didn't like him. I didn't know what to do. I know it was stupid, but you've got to believe there was nothing going on, I can't even understand how you would think such a thing. Surely you know me better than that?"

Rukhsana said nothing and continued to run a finger round and round the top of her mug as she stared at the floor. She wanted to believe Yasmin, but she was filled with doubts and determined not to be made a fool of by anybody. Atiya liked a bit of drama and was inclined to exaggerate, but Rukhsana trusted her and knew she would never lie, especially over something so serious. Could she have just made a mistake in her eagerness to find fault with Yasmin?

"What did Vikram say?" Yasmin asked.

"Don't you know?" Rukhsana was surprised.

"Of course not, I never see him, I told you. I haven't seen him since that day in the snack bar," Yasmin replied vehemently, "I don't ever have anything to do with him."

"No, he said you didn't," Rukhsana murmured. "He also said Atiya got it wrong, he said you asked to see him because you were upset about Sajid and he was trying to reassure you that Sajid did really like you, that's why he held your hand, to console you."

"What a nerve!" Yasmin exclaimed angrily. "I never asked him for anything. He more or less forced me to go for a drink with him!"

"He said loads of different things," Rukhsana sighed. "I could tell he was lying, he's not very good at it, all he did was manage to convince me that Atiya was right and there was something going on. I was so upset with both of you. All I could think was, 'How could Yasmin treat me like this? How could she lie to me?' She looked up and caught Yasmin's eye.

Yasmin looked down at her feet and said quietly, "I'm sorry, I know I should have told you in the first place and it would have stopped all this, but I was trying to save your feelings."

"Well don't next time, please, my feelings don't need that sort of protection," Rukhsana snapped.

"So you believe me now, do you?" Yasmin asked.

"I suppose so," Rukhsana smiled wryly, her expression suddenly softening. "I must admit I can't exactly see it now, it sounded real when Atiya told me, but she does tend to jump to conclusions, especially about you. I suppose I ought to apologise too, I should have listened to you days ago and I'd have known it was just a mix-up." She wanted to give Yasmin a good shake and then hug her tightly until she had crushed out all the pent-up emotions of the last week. But she couldn't move from her seat, she felt stranded across an abyss of sudden shyness and inhibition, hardly trusting herself any more to do or say anything sensible.

"You should've known I wouldn't do anything so stupid," Yasmin reprimanded softly. "What do you think I felt like? Not even being allowed to give you my side of the story?"

"And what do you think I felt like when Atiya told me she'd seen you with Vikram, and you'd just been at my parents' house all weekend and never said a word about it? I felt sick," Rukhsana countered.

"I suppose it must have looked a bit suspicious," Yasmin agreed. "But you could have come and asked me."

"I couldn't bear to talk to you, I was so hurt and angry," Rukhsana replied. "I couldn't see any way that Atiya

151

could be wrong and it just turned everything on its head, all the time I'd been happily thinking that things were one way and then suddenly I turn round and everything's changed and I don't know where I am any more. You should have told me he'd been bothering you."

"I know, I just didn't want to face it really. I felt guilty because I didn't want to have a coffee with him when he first asked me and I knew I should have said no then. So when he held my hand I felt like it was my fault for having got into the situation and for not being stronger. Afterwards I just wanted to forget about it, it felt sort of shameful and I thought if I didn't say anything it would go away."

"Well, you mustn't feel bad about it. He's the one who behaved badly and he lied about it afterwards you know. He's got a lot to explain," Rukhsana muttered sternly.

"Are you going to see him?"

"I told him to stay out of my way, so that's what he'll probably do," Rukhsana replied. "But I think I will try and talk to him again, I want to get things straightened out properly, it would make things a lot easier. The Asian Society meeting last week was awful, apparently."

"Didn't you go?"

"No, I thought you'd be there, and Vikram, so it seemed easier for me to stay away, for all our sakes. In the end it seems none of us went! Shung and Asha got in a right mess with the agenda because half the things on it were things Vikram or I had put down."

"When I was at home this weekend I made a resolution to go to this week's meeting no matter what," Yasmin confided shyly.

"And quite right too!" Rukhsana approved. "It's time more new people got involved, I'm going to have to stop soon, because of Finals, and so are the other third years. You should get stuck in there."

"Do you think I could?" Yasmin asked excitedly.

"Of course," Rukhsana smiled, and then, struck by a worrying thought, said, "Did you tell your Mum about all this?"

"What? When you're supposed to be coming to stay? Certainly not!"

"Just as well or she wouldn't let me in the door!" Rukhsana commented. They both laughed loudly with relief and looked at each other in embarrassment.

"I've been a bit silly, really," Rukhsana said sheepishly. "I could have saved us both a lot of trouble if I'd talked to you on Tuesday, like you wanted. I suppose Sharon and Trish hate me now, if they didn't before."

"I didn't tell them. I didn't tell anyone who knows you, or anyone at home, not even Jenny. The only person I told was Ben."

"Why Ben?"

"I suppose partly because I know he won't tell anyone else, and because he's easy to talk to and he understands about being different and about being mixed up about who you are. You know how you feel safe saying things to some people and not others? And then he knew a bit about what I was talking about because he'd seen Vikram once, in the union bar when we were having a drink after youth club. Oh dear, I didn't tell you about that either."

"No," said Rukhsana, shortly. "Tell me now."

"It wasn't anything. I just went up to the bar to get a drink and Vikram was there as well, getting some drinks for his friends. He asked who I was with and I pointed out Ben. I suppose that's how all this started really, because he assumed I was involved with Ben and he said something stupid about him being Jewish and that I could do better. Up 'till then I didn't even know Ben was Jewish. Anyway, that was it. I didn't like what he said so I got away as soon as possible, I never thought twice about it until the snack bar thing happened, I was much more interested in what Ben and I were talking about that night."

"You must have known I wouldn't like the things Vikram was saying either. Didn't you think you should tell me?"

"I honestly forgot about it 'till I saw him again and then it got so much worse it was like I said before, I didn't want to upset you and I didn't want to think about it."

153

"And look where that got you," Rukhsana commented dryly. "Anyway, never mind now, I don't think I want to hear any more about Vikram. I wish I hadn't told anyone, though, I feel like the whole world knows there's something wrong, everyone keeps asking about me and Vikram and I'm sure Atiya's told them all it's your fault."

"I know, she can't wait to get rid of me," Yasmin muttered sourly. "She more or less said so."

"Have you seen her?" Rukhsana asked looking surprised.

"Yes, didn't she tell you? I went round on Friday morning. That's how I found out it was the coffee bar thing you were upset about."

"Oh, I see," Rukhsana said slowly with growing comprehension. "That was very brave of you."

"Not really," Yasmin demurred. "I didn't know she had anything to do with it, so I wasn't expecting a row. I wanted to see you."

"But it was still pretty brave to come and seek me out in the middle of all my friends and protectors!" Rukhsana laughed. "I don't know if I'd have done it. I bet Atiya gave you a mouthful."

"Yeah. She really hates me, doesn't she?"

"Well, she thinks you're playing around, coming to the society and all that, she thinks you're doing it to be fashionable and when you get bored you'll go back to being with your white friends and forget about us lot. She says you've got a choice about being Asian and we haven't, so it's not the same."   Rukhsana watched Yasmin's face fall and her eyes cloud over with worry and wished she hadn't said that. Yasmin would have to know sometime that Atiya had complained about her being in the group, but maybe now was not the time to raise it.

"But I don't have a real choice," Yasmin protested, strenuously. "It feels kind of inevitable. I know it's not the same, but you don't think it's easier for me, do you?"

"It's not about being easier or harder. It's different for you, having a white mother, but you're not white yourself and even though you didn't know your Dad, it's because of his history and because he was black that you are who you are now. That makes you Asian as far as I'm concerned. I've argued with Atiya about it, she's out on a limb anyway, because most people agree with me and there was never any trouble about Arif or Caroline. She just doesn't like you being so friendly with me."

Yasmin looked doubtful, she had a bit of that old panicky feeling she used to get when having to explain herself to people, that fear of not being taken for who she said she was, wondering what people were really thinking behind their smiling hypocritical eyes.

"Yasmin, you know who you are, you don't have to worry about Atiya, it's just sour grapes because she used to be my best friend," Rukhsana urged her. "Look, why don't you go to Asian Society on your own this week, like you wanted to, and then you'll see how welcome you are. I'll make sure Atiya's cleared up all this stuff about you and Vikram. It'll teach her not to jump in with both feet like that again."

"No, you've got all those things from last week's meeting to sort out, we'll both go," Yasmin insisted. "I know you're right and really I feel fine there, I don't care what Atiya thinks."

"She might not even be at the meeting after I've had a go at her!" Rukhsana commented mischievously.

"Oh no, I don't think you should be too hard on her," Yasmin cautioned, feeling magnanimous.

"You're just an old softy!" Rukhsana teased.

"Maybe. Do you want some more tea?" Yasmin asked, rising from her seat.

"Or we could go out to that Italian place that does the cappuccinos?" Rukhsana suggested, excitedly.

"And the cheesecake and the ice cream!" Yasmin enthused, catching the sparkle in Rukhsana's eyes and luxuriating in the restored warmth of her affection. "Oh yes, you're not too busy, are you?"

"'Course not. I'll go and get organised. Meet you in quarter of an hour," Rukhsana said briskly and hurried out of the room.

It was not quite true to say that she was not too busy, she had saved up a key stage of her fluid mechanics project for tonight, anticipating a need to bury herself in complex technical problems after a short and traumatic meeting with Yasmin. She had expected the meeting to leave a nasty aftertaste like her last meeting with Vikram. Now she would have to do the work later, or tomorrow, but she was glad she had suggested going out, they needed to clear the air and enjoy themselves a bit after the heavy hostile atmosphere of the last week.

On entering her room, Rukhsana stood still, looking around her indecisively. Then she made for the wardrobe and flicked through the clothes, fingering a couple of shirts and a pair of jeans, feeling that the occasion required something special. She looked at herself critically in the mirror and eventually decided that the black shalwar and the mustard-yellow shirt she was wearing would be all right for a restaurant with some different earrings. She felt quite dizzy and light-headed about this whole evening and put it down to her nerves and her wild relief at resolving things and being able to return to their old closeness. She knew now that Yasmin was sincere and she had been a fool to react so unthinkingly to Atiya's poisonous story. 'Yasmin would never have gone charging round to Atiya's house like that to find me if she'd had anything to hide,' she thought, shaking her head affectionately. She was touched to think of Yasmin going round to the house and standing up to Atiya in defence of their friendship. 'She's so much braver than me when it really matters,' she reflected running a brush lightly through the end of her plait and over the stray wisps that fringed her face. Then she switched off the lamp and left the room.

After Rukhsana had gone, Yasmin sat on the bed for a few minutes, savouring her relief that it had turned out all right. The shakiness that she had felt when she returned from dinner and was trying to decide what to do was only just beginning to wear off, and with it the churning hollow feeling in her stomach. She had scarcely eaten anything at dinner and was glad Rukhsana had suggested going out as she was beginning to feel a little hungry. She sighed deeply and dug her chin into her chest as she contemplated the line of books propped against the wall on her desk. The arguments and rivalries she had been through in her seven years' friendship with Jenny seemed petty and muted beside the anguish she had suffered in the last week. Since she had met Rukhsana her life seemed to have become more intense and unpredictable. She was not used to such extremes of emotion and felt somewhat out of her depth, but determined to `hang on in there', as Rod would say.

Thinking of Rod reminded her that she needed to write to Maggie. They had not talked properly again after the conversation on Saturday night that Rod had interrupted, and Yasmin felt that it was up to her to say something, even if it was just to acknowledge that the conversation happened. She made a mental note to start a letter first thing in the morning.

She leaned over the end of the bed and delved in her rucksack for her purse and cheque book, and stuffed them in her blue canvas bag, along with a couple of pens, her diary and a small brush. Then, as an afterthought, she opened the bottom drawer of her desk and under a pile of old letters and packs of photographs, she pulled out the small lacquered jewellery box containing the photo of her parents and herself on a picnic when she was a baby. She had been meaning to show it to Rukhsana for ages, but kept forgetting and now seemed an especially good time to share this treasure from her past.

13

PICTURES OF THE PAST

Rod eased the car into its usual parking space on the road outside the house.

"You two go in, I'll bring the luggage," he said, switching the headlights off and turning to Rukhsana seated beside him. "Maggie'll be going spare about the food, she started ages ago."

"Okay," Yasmin agreed from the back, opening her door. She was feeling ridiculously nervous and half wished she could see Maggie alone first. Rukhsana got out too and Yasmin led her down the narrow passage to the shared back yard. The yard was very dark as there were no street lamps at the back of the house, just the pool of light shed from the kitchen window. The clouds banked in the sky above were tinged with a faint orange glow from the myriad lights in the valley below. A cold wind whipped across the yard lifting Rukhsana's loose hair and swirling it around her shoulders and face. She brushed it back with one hand and gasped, "It's really high up here, isn't it?"

"Just a bit!" Yasmin replied, with a hint of pride. "Come on in, it's freezing out here, you'll see the view tomorrow."

They stumbled into the warm, brightly lit kitchen, the wind chasing after them in angry gusts. Maggie was standing by the cooker, anxiously watching over a collection of simmering pans.

"Hello! What took you so long?" she exclaimed with relief as they came in.

"The train was late and it was really packed. We had to stand in the corridor," Yasmin explained, kissing her mother. Then, ushering Rukhsana forward, she announced, somewhat superfluously, "Mum, meet Rukhsana. Rukhsana, this is my Mum."

"Call me Maggie, it's nice to meet you," Maggie smiled.

"I hope the rice hasn't got too dry, it's been in the oven for ages, it's a pilau, won't be as nice as your mother's."

"It smells wonderful," Rukhsana sniffed appreciatively. "We couldn't get near the buffet on the train, so we're ravenous."

"Good, well I'll lay the table. Yasmin, why don't you make a cup of tea, I'm sure you're both gasping. Sit down, Rukhsana."

Rukhsana sat at the table while Yasmin rattled out the cups, chatting busily to fill the cautious silence between Maggie and Rukhsana. Soon she had to leave the tea-making to Rukhsana while she helped Rod carry their rucksacks and travel bags upstairs to the attic.

"Yasmin's always talking about you," Maggie said to Rukhsana when they were alone. "She really values your opinions."

"She's always talking about you too," Rukhsana responded breezily.

"Well, we have our ups and downs as you've heard, no doubt," Maggie said, pointedly.

Rukhsana concentrated on pouring the tea, not sure how to respond.

"She said she had a lovely time when she went home with you," Maggie continued. "I suppose she feels she's missed out on the kind of life you have at home, you know, a big family, speaking your own language, knowing about your religion and where you've come from, all that sort of stuff."

"Oh no, I don't think so," Rukhsana replied earnestly. "I think she's really satisfied with her life. She's always telling me what a happy teenager she was compared to most of her friends. She's just taking on new interests now and moving forward, that doesn't mean she regrets anything that happened before, I don't think. But why don't you ask her?"

"I do..." Maggie looked across at Rukhsana sceptically and was going to say more, but Yasmin and Rod clattered down the stairs. She and Rukhsana both turned back guiltily to what they were supposed to be doing.

They all sat down to eat around the big kitchen table, with its red-checked plastic tablecloth. They chatted about the end of term for students and for departmental secretaries respectively, Maggie complaining it was no vacation for her with all the work the lecturers had piled on for the next term. Rod was interested in the burden placed on the rail network by thousands of students all flooding the trains at the same time, as they made their various ways home across the country.

"They should stagger the holidays or put more carriages on the trains," he opined, indignantly. "It's not right you girls having to stand for nearly two hours."

"Young women," Yasmin corrected teasing him. "You're not much of a youth worker, are you?"

"I know, but it's different when it's you, you're still Maggie's girl to me!" Rod laughed unapologetically. "Anyway, as I was saying, they must know it's going to happen the last Friday of every term and they never do anything about it. When I was in India the more reservations there were, the more carriages they put on, simple as that, it was a model of efficiency. The British have just forgotten how to run a railway system."

"When were you in India?" Rukhsana interrupted curiously.

"Oh, in my hippy youth," Rod replied looking slightly embarrassed. "I don't think you'd approve, I smoked a lot of dope and cluttered up the beaches of Goa in a most insensitive fashion, I'm not very proud of it now."

"Did you go overland?" Rukhsana asked.

"Yeah, six of us in an old truck, you can't do it now of course, drive through Iran and Afghanistan, but it was a brilliant experience..." Rod noticed Maggie looking at him sharply and broke off.

"My uncle used to get a lot of overlanders coming into his cafe, he was on the Grand Trunk Road in Lahore," Rukhsana commented, remembering old family stories. "He thought most of them were filthy and bad-mannered, I think they were a bit of a joke to most people."

"A bit of a joke to ourselves as well," Rod said good-humouredly. "I was in India for six months once we got there, I'd love to go back now and see what it's all like, but it costs so much and..."

"And I'm not keen," Maggie interrupted, looking uncomfortable, "I don't really like travelling and I've never been in an aeroplane, I don't fancy it much."

"Really?" Rukhsana looked surprised.

"Have you actually talked about going to India?" Yasmin said, looking from Maggie to Rod, in astonishment. This appeared to be an on-going discussion she had never been part of.

"Not seriously," Maggie replied dismissively. "Rod has these wild fantasies sometimes, thinks he's twenty-one again and can travel the world. What about some more rice, Rukhsana?"

"I never said the world, just India," Rod said quietly.

"Why didn't you say anything to me? We could all three go together," Yasmin persisted, feeling a rising sense of outrage that they could have excluded her from this important discussion so casually. She knew she had never taken any interest in Rod's travelling tales before. Until this term, India had just been a geography topic that left her with a sour taste. But it was the country out of which Pakistan had been born and if she had known they were talking about travelling there, she might have thought of a lot of things much sooner...

"I didn't think you'd want to go with us," Maggie replied firmly. "You'll probably want to go with someone your own age one day. Anyway, it's all a bit pie in the sky when we're not even sure we can afford to go to Scotland next year, so let's talk about something else, shall we? What do you two want to do tomorrow morning?"

"I'm dying to see this countryside Yasmin's always talking about," Rukhsana suggested brightly. "She thinks we don't have any in the south-east!"

"Count me out, I've got a report to write," Rod replied, leaning back expansively.

"Go on, Mum, you'll come for a walk with us, won't you?" Yasmin urged her.

"Well, the car won't drive itself there, will it?" Maggie laughed reluctantly. "But I must get some shopping in first, you'll probably be asleep 'till all hours anyway, knowing what you're like in the holidays! Rod, get a tin of peaches out of the cupboard, will you?"

She began gathering up the plates.

The next day was grey and subdued. They set off briskly from the car, following a twisting muddy path that ran alongside a small stream tumbling headlong over mossy boulders into sudden green pools. On either side rose steep wooded hillsides, thick with rowan and birch trees and old pines whose bare trunks towered skywards in haphazard colonnades, their topmost branches forming a ragged canopy of dark coniferous green. The ground was carpeted in old brown needles and dead leaves. Rukhsana had to watch her footing all the time to avoid tripping over stones and gnarled tree roots embedded in the slippery path. Maggie went first and Yasmin followed, chatting desultorily. Rukhsana walked at the back listening to the liquid burble of the stream and breathing in the fresh chill air, smelling of damp vegetation and pine trees. The strong sweet scent of the pines suddenly stopped her in her tracks, and she half-closed her eyes for a moment as she was transported way back to what seemed like another life. She was on holiday with her uncle and cousins in a hill station near Islamabad. She could see sunlight filtering through dense pine trees and a thunderous swollen white river rushing through the forest, its roar drowning her terrified scream. She remembered her uncle catching hold of her and scolding her for going too near the water, and hiding her head in his rough warm shawl as he lifted her up to comfort her...

"Are you okay, Rukhsana?" Yasmin's voice broke into her thoughts and she saw that they had turned round and were looking at her anxiously.

"Yes, I'm fine!" she breathed laughing. "It's the smell of the pine trees, it just took me right back to when I was

162

little and went on holiday once to the hills. It's exactly the same smell, it's amazing! and it looked a bit like this too, really steep and lots of tall trees, I never thought there was anywhere so like Pakistan in this country."

"That's funny, it always reminds us of Scotland, doesn't it, Mum?"

"Yes. Let's sit down a minute," Maggie suggested, picking her way over to a cluster of boulders by the stream. Rukhsana followed gratefully, a little shaken by the sudden return of a memory buried so deeply. She was seized by an overwhelming and totally impractical longing to return immediately and seek out that exact spot by the river where she had strayed from her uncle's side.

"I remember Yasmin's father talking about a place in the hills he used to go to on holiday, somewhere called Murree, I think," Maggie said to Rukhsana.

"Oh yes, maybe that's where it was," Rukhsana replied eagerly. "I'll ask my Mum."

"We went on a picnic to the South Downs with some friends," Maggie remembered. "And it was just like with you just now, Rukhsana. Farooq was really thrown by something in the air. The sunshine and suddenly being out of London after years of living in the city took him right back to Pakistan. It affected him for days, made him really nostalgic."

"I bet he wanted to take you there and show you how beautiful it is," Rukhsana said gently.

"Yes, he did actually," Maggie replied, startled by the exactness with which Rukhsana had guessed Farooq's words. "What makes you say that?"

"Just because it is so beautiful, we're very proud of it, and when you love people you want to share important things like that with them, don't you?" Rukhsana and Maggie looked at each other briefly and intently and Yasmin remained quiet. It mattered to her very much that the two of them should like each other. But now she felt them drawing together over rosy memories of Pakistan that were not even Maggie's own, she felt speechlessly angry with both of them. She looked at her mother's rapt, emotional expression and thought, `It's taken her fifteen years to begin to tell me anything about my father. How can she slip so easily into sharing all these memories with Rukhsana the first time they meet? It's not right, he's my father. She should be talking to me about it all and I should be the one to tell Rukhsana, if I want to.'

"Anyway, in the end he wasn't interested in sharing any of it," Maggie said bitterly, looking away. "He didn't share much at all, I've come to realise. Maybe he thought we weren't good enough for his precious Pakistan?"

"Or maybe he was scared Pakistan wouldn't be good enough for you?" Rukhsana suggested hesitantly. "After all, most white people think it's not good enough for them, don't they?"

"Well, he should have known me better," Maggie argued passionately. "I would have gone and lived there if he'd asked me. I was a different person then, you know. I would have gone anywhere with him. But he didn't even trust me enough to discuss it with me. Did he think I wouldn't understand?"

"I don't know, I'm not him," Rukhsana reminded her.

"I know, I'm sorry, love," Maggie apologised, her face softening. "I didn't mean it was anything to do with you, I know you can't speak for him any more than I can."

"It's all right," Rukhsana interrupted lightly. "I think Yasmin's got a photo of that picnic. Isn't it the one you showed me last week, Yasmin?"

Yasmin murmured assent, looking away from them across the stream.

"Yasmin? Are you all right?" Maggie pursued, anxiously, seeing the disapproval written on her daughter's firmly turned back.

"Fine," Yasmin replied with defiant sarcasm. "I mean, it's really great to hear about that picnic now, after I've carried the photo around for so many years and never knew anything about it."

"I'll tell you what," Maggie said, forcing an air of cheerfulness. "When we get back, I'll get out all the old photos for us to look at and we can show them to Rukhsana. It's time I sorted them out properly. I think there may even be some your father left that he brought from Pakistan - he left so much stuff like that. I suppose maybe he did think he was coming back - I've even got his degree certificate somewhere. I just put it all in boxes and left it."

"What boxes?" Yasmin swung round angrily. "You never told me there were any boxes!"

"They're in the shed. I thought I did tell you, love. That's where I fetched the photos from when I showed them to you."

"But I didn't know there were any more. You never said anything about boxes. Why didn't you throw it away?" Yasmin asked her, remembering how much Maggie had hated any mention of Farooq over the years.

"I really don't know, I suppose I was saving it for posterity or whatever, I was never very good at letting go."

"Just as well, or I wouldn't have anything now," Yasmin muttered grimly.

"Hadn't we better carry on? I'm sure you're used to walking further than this," Rukhsana prompted, and they all rose and continued in a straggly line up the path.

At the top of the small valley, the path wound away from the stream and up a steep slithery bank out onto the level, heather-covered moors above. When they had all scrambled to the top they stood for a while, admiring the view over the muted wintry greens and browns of the massed treetops. Below the wooded slopes lay the reservoir's steel-grey sheet of water, cut off at one end by the clean line of the dam wall. Beyond, a broad valley, flanked by barren fields and lowering purple crags, stretched back into the distant grey blur of the city. A light wind was beginning to blow up again, tearing at the frayed edges of the solid cloud banks above and rustling in the pine boughs. Yasmin forgot her anger for a moment in the warm pride and satisfaction she felt at seeing the undulating hills and soft autumnal colours. She wanted to show Rukhsana every last brown, dry frond of bracken and craggy grey rock as if they were all part of herself.

Rukhsana breathed in the faint evocative scent of pine trees again, she was aware of a pleasing tiredness in her limbs and felt quite proud of her performance. But she was anxious about Yasmin, knowing that something was wrong from the unusual flash of hostility she had shown earlier.

"It's back down the same way, I'm afraid," Maggie said to her. "How did you find the climb?"

"Fine, it wasn't too tiring at all, I must be fitter than I thought," Rukhsana replied cheerfully.

"I bet it doesn't look like Pakistan up here," Yasmin commented, looking out over the wide valley to the dark purple moors on the far horizon.

"Certainly not, everything's too small and the sky's too grey," Rukhsana replied laughing. "I wish you could both come with me to Pakistan sometime, we could stay with my relatives in Lahore."

"We could even see if we could get some news about my Dad," Yasmin speculated, excitedly. The world suddenly seemed to shrink and Lahore was transformed from some remote place in childhood mythology to a city as ordinary and accessible as London or Paris.

"Oh no," Maggie said, in tones of horror. "Not for me, I'm not dragging all that up again after fifteen years, I'm sorry. It would just be too upsetting. Besides, it could cause a lot of trouble, you might ruin some other family's life."

"Oh well, if it would be too upsetting for you we couldn't do it, never mind what anyone else wants!" Yasmin burst out vehemently. "I don't believe this! All this time I never asked you about the past because I didn't want to hurt you, but it doesn't upset you to tell other people about him, does it? And what about me being upset not knowing anything? You should have told me all this stuff years ago, you just couldn't be bothered!"

"That's not true..." Maggie tried to interrupt, but Yasmin carried on furiously. "And why didn't you talk about going to India with me. You and Rod have obviously been thinking of it for years. And now I find out there are whole boxes of my Dad's stuff that have been sitting in the back yard all these years and I never knew about them! How could you not tell me? You said you didn't know about him, you said he didn't leave anything, you always made me feel there was nothing worth finding out, he was just a waste of space. But you didn't throw his stuff away, did you? So you must have still loved him. It's all been lies!" She swept away down the path, calling back incoherently, "I'm going back to the car!"

"Yasmin, wait a minute!" Maggie called desperately, but Yasmin strode on determinedly, leaving her mother and Rukhsana standing helplessly in stunned silence.

"You go ahead, I'll be all right," Rukhsana said at length. Maggie glanced up at her distractedly and then set off after Yasmin's fast disappearing figure.

As Yasmin stormed down the hillside, her mind raced over the many injustices which suddenly seemed to surround her. When she had shown Rukhsana that photo she had told her that Maggie didn't remember where it was taken. She had believed Maggie when she said she had put it out of her mind years ago. Now it seemed she had forgotten nothing and thrown nothing away. Yasmin shook her head in disbelief at the thought of the innocuous grey shed door she had passed countless times a day ever since she could remember, concealing keys to her past that she could have rummaged through whenever she liked if she had known. A flicker of doubt crossed her mind. Maybe she had been told but had not been interested at the time? `But that's not the point,' she thought. `Whether or not I was interested, Mum should have encouraged me to find out more things so I could have chosen whether or not to be interested.' She heard a twig crack loudly some distance behind her and looked back to see Maggie hurrying down the path. Sighing, she turned round and waited for her to catch up.

"What have you done with Rukhsana?" she asked wryly, when Maggie reached her.

"She's coming..." Maggie paused to catch her breath and then continued, "Look, love, I'm sorry you're so upset about all this, but everything I did was to try and protect you."

"Oh?" Yasmin looked sceptical and carried on walking down the path. She almost said, "Or was it to protect yourself?" but bit back the words.

"Yes," Maggie insisted, urgently, falling in step beside her. "How could I encourage you to get all fired up about your father, when I knew you could never see him or have any contact with him? When you were little I just wanted you to be happy and not wishing for things you couldn't have. I thought it was better to let things be. I suppose I just lost track of how quickly you were growing up."

"But you should have told me about my Dad and Pakistan, and all that stuff of his. You can't make difficult things go away by not talking about them, you know."

"Yes, I do know," Maggie retorted, sharply. "Don't speak to me as if I'm a child. I may have made mistakes but I'm still your mother."

"Sorry," Yasmin muttered. "But you don't understand how difficult you've made it for me, running away from it all this time. I've been in a real mess this term trying to catch up with all the things I should have been learning about for the last eighteen years. And you've hidden things from me, like you never said Rod wanted you to go to India."

"I've already said, it was never a serious discussion, and it was between Rod and me. Like a lot of the stuff about your Dad is really between him and me. It's private. I had a right not to discuss it if I didn't want to. Parents have their own relationships that are their business and nothing to do with their children..."

"Okay, but some of it was to do with him being my father and me being half-Pakistani. I should have known about all those bits."

"All right," Maggie agreed, turning to Yasmin as they reached the car. "I agree you should. But you never gave me any sign that it meant anything to you. You never asked about your father, or Pakistan..."

"I always felt like I shouldn't ask, it seemed like you never wanted it mentioned."

"So, what do you want me to do now? I've started to tell you things, haven't I?"

"You could try and understand why it's so important to me," Yasmin replied, passionately. "You think it's all to do with my Dad, but it isn't, not really. Its about knowing where I've come from and why I'm Asian when you're white"

"But I can't know what that feels like, can I?" Maggie said softly, with pain in her voice. She was leaning against a wall at the side of the road and Yasmin was perched on the car bonnet facing her.

"But that's what I mean!" Yasmin replied, excitedly. "That's what I want you to understand. Before, you said we're all the same and you didn't see what the problem was. But now can't you see it is different for me, and that's good. It's great, I like being Asian. I just want to know more about it, that's all."

They saw Rukhsana approaching, dawdling her way down the path towards the last gate.

"We should try not to make a scene in front of Rukhsana," Maggie commented. "It's not fair, it's not her fault."

"Oh honestly, Mum, she knows about it all anyway. Let's just try and sort it out so there aren't any more scenes."

"Yes, well you'll just have to be patient with me. I'm only your stupid old mother," Maggie frowned, unlocking the car door. "I never went to university."

"Don't be silly," Yasmin retorted impatiently, jumping off the bonnet. "You know it's not about passing exams. You might never agree with me, I just want you to understand what I'm saying."

Rukhsana's arrival cut short further discussion. On the way home Maggie concentrated on driving, while Rukhsana and Yasmin sat in the back in awkward silence. From time to time Rukhsana glanced across at Yasmin's pensive expression, trying to guage her mood. Eventually, she reached over and squeezed Yasmin's hand sympathetically. A look of gentle understanding passed between them and Yasmin smiled back at her gratefully.

After lunch Maggie kept her promise and brought a couple of dusty cardboard boxes in from the outhouse, where she kept stuff she never needed, but couldn't bear to throw away. They were dry, but so dirty she had to put them on newspaper on the kitchen floor and dust them thoroughly before she would let Yasmin and Rukhsana near them.

She watched the old text books and foolscap files come out, one after another, hundreds of pages of faded notes and drafts that Farooq had pored over night after night in his cramped digs. The surprising thing was she felt no pain, it was more of a release to see these old things passed around and thumbed through. They became familiar and mundane again, whereas hidden away they had assumed an oppressive importance to her.

If she had been allowed to choose, she might have decided, as she always did, that they were best left where they were. But for some weeks now, Yasmin had been prising open everything that Maggie had so carefully sealed up over the years. It had begun with that tentative letter, mentioning that she had been thinking about her father. Now, the tide seemed unstoppable, even to the point of wanting to go to Pakistan with Rukhsana. 'Opening these boxes is just part of the whole thing,' Maggie thought, with wary resignation. 'Though where it's going to end, I don't know...'

"Look, here are the photos," Yasmin cried, taking out a thick paper wallet of photos from the second box and turning it over reverently.

"Let's take them in the other room, we can sit more comfortably," Maggie suggested, and they followed her through to the front room and sat in a line on the settee with Yasmin in the middle holding the wallet of photos. Some of them she remembered seeing before, but right at

the back of the wallet, Yasmin discovered some old black
and white photos of her father as a boy.

"Those are the ones I was talking about," Maggie said
uneasily. "The ones he brought from Pakistan. I knew I'd
seen them somewhere."

They all craned forward to see the small boy standing
stiffly in front of a heavy wooden door, squinting at the
sun. In another photo there was a family group of the
same small boy, two other boys and what appeared to be
their parents, all posing in the foreground. Behind them,
in the distance, there rose a towering pointed monument
with a base of unfolding petals of stone.

"I know where that is!" Rukhsana cried when she saw it.
"It's in Lahore, it's the Minar-e-Pakistan, look, it's meant
to be like a lotus bud and it symbolises the birth of
Pakistan, or something. We went there when I was little.
And that one looks like the Shalimar Bagh." She pointed
to another family pose in a park before cascading
fountains. "That's near where my uncle had his
restaurant!"

"How amazing that you know where they are!" Yasmin
breathed, overwhelmed at the sight of these passports into
another world that was at the same time a part of herself.
The sense she had of reaching out was almost tangible
and she stared at the pictures as though she wanted to
step into them. Turning to Maggie, she asked eagerly,
"Are they my grandparents then, Mum?"

"I think they must be," Maggie replied uncertainly,
picking up one of the photos and studying it helplessly.
"I'm afraid I don't know for sure. I don't remember him
actually showing these to me, he just kept them in his
desk and I found them when I was packing to leave
London. Still, it's nice to have someone look at them who
can appreciate where they're taken at least," and she
smiled at Rukhsana and passed the photo back to Yasmin.
They all peered at the three little boys in long khaki
trousers, the small serious-looking woman enveloped in a
large shawl, and the stern dignified figure at the back,
with his finely trimmed moustache and white topi

perched on his balding head. Yasmin remembered that the man was now dead and tried to take this in, but her emotions were in turmoil. Her mind leapt ahead, crazily, and she imagined herself standing in the blinding midday sun outside a heavy wooden door like the one in the first photograph. She imagined the door opening to reveal the small, serious woman, older and greyer and wrapped in a white shawl. "Assalaam alaikum," she imagined herself saying, "Mai Yasmin huu." In a way she knew it did not matter if she never received a response, if she never met her father or his mother. The important thing was the journey, to try, to go, to seek out the connections. Echoes of herself were calling out to her from these old discoloured photographs and she needed to follow them.

14
LASTING CONNECTION

Rukhsana gazed into the purring gas fire as her thoughts wandered back over the day's events. They were all gathered in the drowsy warmth of the living room after dinner. Maggie was watching a murder mystery on television. Rod and Yasmin were struggling with The Guardian crossword, arguing over synonyms and obscure references to Greek mythology. Rukhsana was supposed to be watching the television too, but her thoughts were drifting back to the morning's walk, the row before lunch, and the fragile afternoon spent healing rifts and unearthing dusty treasures from the past in old boxes on the kitchen floor. The walk had made real all those photos of mountains and moorland on Yasmin's walls in college, and had filled Rukhsana with a strange restlessness. She felt closer to the sky here, in this small house clinging to the ancient wind-buffeted hillside. And closer to those long-buried memories of Pakistan, the chill mist in the mountains at dawn, fires at dusk, the lights of distant villages twinkling across deep yawning valleys. She wondered what it must feel like for Yasmin seeing those photographs and yet never having been to Pakistan, thinking of Scotland rather than Kashmir when she smelt the pine trees.

`If we saved up from now, I could take her next summer, after my finals,' Rukhsana thought, glancing affectionately at Yasmin's bowed head poring over the small print of the newspaper. She wanted to share Yasmin's excitement when she first stepped out into the dusty suffocating heat of Karachi, or the dazzling blue skies of Islamabad. When she had first met Yasmin she had seen her as rather young and unformed. `But I was wrong,' she thought admiringly. `She's worked things out so fast, and faced things head on that lots of people run away from all their lives. She's always moving, asking questions, even when she's got no idea where they'll lead. That's what I love about her, she's so open...'

Her thoughts were interrupted by Maggie turning to her companionably and saying, "It's got to be the secretary, don't you think? She's too perfect...and she knew about the manuscript."

"Oh, I can never work these things out, the clues are so ridiculous," Rukhsana replied hastily, realising she hadn't been paying attention. "I probably blinked at the vital moment!"

"It's the brother, actually," Rod murmured, with casual confidence, looking up from the paper.

"You're not even watching it!" Yasmin protested.

"Well, that's just like a man, isn't it?" Maggie retorted in a disparaging tone. "Passing judgment on things he knows nothing about! Stick to your crossword and leave us in peace, Rod."

Rod settled down to the paper again with a pretence of being ruffled, and Yasmin and Rukhsana exchanged amused smiles. Their eyes held for a moment and Yasmin felt suddenly shy at the tenderness she saw in Rukhsana's smile. There seemed to be a buzzing, tingling feeling in the air, like an invisible charge connecting them across the unwitting ordinariness of the room. Sometimes she thought she was imagining it, but increasingly she felt a new atmosphere of suspense between them, as if they were teetering on the brink of something. Rukhsana turned to the television screen again and Yasmin continued to watch her thoughtfully. Two weeks ago she could not have imagined this and she took warm pleasure in seeing Rukhsana comfortably ensconced in their front room, as if she had been there all her life. She was dreading their parting on Monday and wondered if there was any way of prolonging Rukhsana's stay. She felt so intense and alive when she was with her that the thought of the intervening weeks before her own return to university weighed her down unbearably. All she could see ahead was an agony of waiting and dragging time.

`Maybe I could go back early after Chri[s]
thought suddenly. `God, Yasmin, you're a g[
smiled to herself and looked across
speculatively.

"Mum?" she began, leaping in boldly. "I wa[
going back early after Christmas. I really nee[
library and I've got loads of extra work t[
exams in May."

Rukhsana looked at her in surprise and said[

"Can't you use the library here?" Maggie
her eyes still fixed on the television screen.

"I could, but the departmental library's g[
and I'll probably work better down the[
explained.

"Okay, love, if that's what you want," M[
easily. "I'll be going back to work after Chris[
Oh look! They're going to tell us who did it!"

They all gazed intently at the televisio[
dramatic scene unfolded. It was revea[
murderer had been neither the secretary n[
but the wife herself, secretly in league with t[

"Mmm...I enjoyed that," Maggie said,[
stretching as the closing titles rolled up on[
there anything else on tonight worth watchi[

Rod flicked through the paper till [
television page and scoured it carefully.

"The News...uh...there's a Clint Eastw[
another film's just started on Four, t[
performance of the Messiah from..."

"What's the other film about?" Maggi[
interested.

"It says here, `...Graduate son, Phil, bring[
Chris, home from college to meet the paren[
as it appears when Chris turns out to [
sensitive portrayal of the effect of a gay re[
middle American family.' Sounds ver[
worthy to me," Rod concluded, critically.

"What do you mean?" Yasmin as[
immediately of Ben.

Nothing really," Rod shrugged, looking surprised at sharpness of her tone. "It just sounds a bit heavy for a urday night. You know, the sort of thing we know we ht to care about, but not on my day off, please."

What, like racism?" Yasmin flashed back.

d stared at her, shocked.

He just means he wants some light entertainment," ggie intervened, soothingly. "We've got nothing inst gays and lesbians or anything like that. It's ple's own business what they do, but we don't have to ch it on our screens, do we?"

Vhy not? We watch enough heterosexual sex all the e. It's in adverts and films and everything. It might do ood to see something different," Yasmin argued.

o you think your Mum and I need educating, do ?" Rod turned to her, mildly amused.

just don't think oppression stops at five o'clock when leave work," Yasmin countered stubbornly.

Did I say that?" Rod asked, lifting an eyebrow cently.

top it, you two," Maggie said firmly. "He's just in a d because he wants to watch Clint Eastwood, and seen it a dozen times before. Let's catch the News and decide what else to watch later. Or we can play a e or something..."

ctually, we could go upstairs and listen to some ic, couldn't we, Yasmin?" Rukhsana suggested, ing at Yasmin inquiringly.

o, come on, it's your weekend, the two of you. You watch what you like, don't mind me," Rod insisted, -humouredly.

s all right, really," Yasmin let out an impatient sigh. d rather go upstairs for a bit. We'll come down for a later on."

hatever you want," Maggie agreed. "See you later." watched them retreat through the door and then d at Rod anxiously.

ere's something going on with those two, I can feel ish Yasmin would tell me, she's so jumpy."

"What's your theory, Miss Marple?" Rod asked, jokingly.

"Trust you not to take it seriously."

"Well, I don't think either of them is pregnant..." Rod continued speculating. "And I don't think they're having any secret affairs with married men, or other such undesirables..."

"Of course not, Yasmin's too sensible and she'd tell me. No, it's something between the two of them..." Maggie paused, lost in thought. "She's really grown up this term, and she's so definite about what she thinks now. I should be proud of her, shouldn't I?"

"She's a strong young woman," Rod affirmed, seriously. "But she's got to realise she's not always right, and other people's feelings matter too. I mean, you were in a real state when you got back this morning."

"Well, that's been coming a long time and I should have done something about it before it got to this stage. I don't blame her, she's going through a lot of changes at the moment. But she certainly put you in your place just now," she smiled mischievously.

"Yes, she was very touchy about it, wasn't she?" Rod said, with a puzzled frown.

"Rukhsana ought to be in the Diplomatic Corps, with the amount she's had to put up with from the three of us today. I can't imagine what she thinks."

"You've changed your tune, haven't you?"

"I know. Well, actually, I like her. I just worry about what's going to happen when she's not there anymore. Yasmin thinks so much of her. Still, it's no use me saying anything," she sighed, deeply. "I was thinking about asking Rukhsana if she wants to stay on longer. What you do think?"

"Oh, definitely," Rod agreed. "She's a nice kid, and Yasmin would love it."

"For goodness' sake, don't call her a kid or you'll start something else," Maggie laughed and then added, "Go and put the kettle on, love, and we'll all have a drink in a bit."

"Sorry about that," Yasmin laughed when they reached the attic. "I seem to be picking a lot of fights today." She walked over to the desk and began shuffling through her tapes.

Rukhsana sat on the bed watching her. "No need to be sorry, you were right," she said, approvingly.

"Well, I didn't mean to have another argument," Yasmin said, swinging round in exasperation. "It's just that Rod thinks he's so right on because he goes on all these awareness courses. And then he comes out with stuff like that!"

"He seems to think it's just to do with work, doesn't he?" Rukhsana leant back on her elbows as Yasmin continued, indignantly. "Exactly! They both assume it's got nothing to do with them! But how do they know they don't work with someone gay every day? Come to that, how do they know that I'm not...I mean, I could fall for another woman, couldn't I?" she faltered, looking at Rukhsana with sudden intensity.

There was a hushed, loaded silence and Rukhsana got up and walked over to the desk. She ran her thumb nail along a small crack in the wood, the tiny noise scratching at the taut silence in the room.

"What are you saying, Yasmin?"

"I don't know," Yasmin half-whispered, searching Rukhsana's calm face for some clue as to her thoughts. "Nothing in particular...I mean I was just making a general point really. Oh God, I think I'm just messing things up again. Forget I spoke." She looked down at her fingers desperately twisting the last button of her shirt. She wished she could claw back her foolish words, pretend they never happened. It was so easy to ruin everything. She felt weak with despair. Then Rukhsana's hands were suddenly touching hers, stilling their distracted movement. She drew in a quick breath of surprise and looked up to meet Rukhsana's steady, passionate gaze.

"What...?"

"Sshh..." Rukhsana silenced her. She let go of Yasmin's hands and pulled her in close, hugging her tightly. Yasmin shut her eyes and buried her face in Rukhsana's thick, tumbling hair, feeling her heart beat through her thin shirt and solid warmth of her body. Her fingers clung to the cardigan on Rukhsana's back and she breathed in the scent of her skin and the fresh coconut oil smell of her washed hair. Her mind was racing over things they had said before, things Ben had said, and Atiya, past moments of near intimacy and pulling back. In all those moments she had never dared to imagine this and now it felt so right and natural. Above the feverish clamour of her thoughts, she felt the cool clear touch of certainty and knew that this was where she wanted to be. They held each other for what seemed like many minutes until Yasmin finally moved back a little and looked tentatively at Rukhsana.

"Does this mean we feel the same?" she breathed, disbelievingly.

"I think so," Rukhsana answered, her voice shaking slightly. They stood still, looking at each other in shy amazement, and a gentle silence fell on the room.

"Come on, let's sit down," Rukhsana whispered, moving to a corner. They settled down on an old floor cushion, Yasmin enfolded in Rukhsana's arms, her head resting against Rukhsana's shoulder. For a while they remained quiet. Yasmin could feel Rukhsana's warm breath against her hair. She wanted to stay there forever, enveloped in this safe precious moment, just the two of them, it felt so complete.

"I can't believe it, I was so scared you didn't feel the same," she murmured at length, entwining her fingers in Rukhsana's soft hair.

"Oh, I knew what was happening alright, but I was really scared too."

They laughed a little thinking of all the meaningful looks that had passed between them lately, looks understood but not acknowledged.

"Would you have said something if I hadn't?" Yasmin

asked, curiously.

"I don't know," Rukhsana laughed, shaking her head. "I'm such a coward sometimes. I would probably have gone back on Monday in the same tizz I've been in for the last two weeks and been totally frustrated and miserable! I've been in a muddle ever since I realised I made a total mistake with Vikram..."

"How do you mean?"

"Well, I'd been looking in the wrong place, hadn't I? Too stupid to see the obvious right under my nose."

"I think I first realised properly after I had that row with Atiya," Yasmin said, thinking back. "When she said how much you talked about me...I was so excited about that!"

"God, she'd be furious if she knew! She worked so hard to split us up!"

"Because she probably fancies you herself!"

"Yasmin! That's wicked!" Rukhsana pushed her teasingly in the ribs.

"Wicked but true," Yasmin laughed. "Anyway, she doesn't have to know. It's none of her business, or anyone else's."

"I can't imagine what they're all going to say back at college, can you?" Rukhsana said, running a hand through her loose hair in a relaxed, self-satisfied gesture.

"I know one person who'll be wild about it!" Yasmin smiled to herself. "In fact, I think he knew about it before I did!"

"Who?" Rukhsana was intrigued.

"My friend Ben. He told me to `go for it' ages back, but I didn't really understand what he meant. He's gay, you see. I shouldn't really tell you, but I don't think he'll mind now that we're - you know - together." She laughed awkwardly, fumbling for a form of words.

Rukhsana squeezed her gently, sharing the feeling of newness and stepping into uncharted territory.

"I might tell my aunty Farida, I wonder what she'd say," she mused, thinking of her childhood heroine. "She's so strong and independent, I'm sure it's her influence that's made me like I am. But I don't know how she'd take it if I said so, we don't really have conversations like that. I think she feels she has to be quite careful not to get on the wrong side of my parents."

"I'd love to meet her," Yasmin commented.

"Hey, yes!" Rukhsana cried, enthusiastically. "We could go and see her one weekend in term-time. Honestly, I've thought of so many plans for after Christmas, my mind's just been buzzing with them and wondering what you'd think of them! It was really funny when you asked your Mum about going back early because I'd been thinking about it myself, but I wasn't sure you'd be able to leave her so soon."

"I was surprised she said okay myself. I haven't the foggiest how I'll wangle it though. My room's only booked from the last weekend of the holiday."

"That's no problem, you can stay with me, they'll never know!" Rukhsana winked mischievously. "Just think, all that time together and no-one else around to bother us. It'll be so good!"

"But what about your work?"

"What am I going to do down there on my own, except mooch around all day thinking about you? I'll never concentrate, not that I will if you're with me either, but at least we'll be together not concentrating!" They hugged, laughing, and kissed each other softly, their eyes closed, lips brushing across cheeks and nuzzling gently into each other's necks to rest for a long moment in a warm tender embrace.

"What else have you been thinking then and not telling me?" Yasmin whispered, in a gently chiding tone, moving back to look at Rukhsana with mock severity.

"Well," Rukhsana began blithely, "I thought at Easter we could go away to a cottage for a week when I'm revising for finals. Then there's the Pakistan trip for next summer, or maybe Christmas when the weather's much better. Also, I've more or less decided to stay on after finals and do voluntary advice work. I thought I'd look for a flat or a bedsit...or we could even look together, but it's all just ideas, you know..."

"Brilliant ideas," Yasmin enthused warmly and was about to say more when Maggie's voice from below startled them apart.

"Yasmin! Rukhsana! Do you want a drink?" she called.

"Oh! Yes please! We're just coming!" Yasmin yelled back, stifling her giggles as she caught a glance of wicked amusement from Rukhsana. "Is that okay?" she whispered.

"Of course. We should try and be sociable," Rukhsana replied in a low voice. "It's only fair to your Mum."

"I don't know what she'd say if she knew about all this," Yasmin responded, dubiously.

"She'd think I was a wicked older woman trying to whisk you away to Pakistan," Rukhsana shrugged, cheerfully. "Come on, let's get these drinks. She stood up and as she moved towards the stairs, Yasmin caught her sleeve and gently pulled her back, saying with quiet assurance, "Hang on a minute. What about another hug?" She looked at Rukhsana's dark eyes and smiling mouth, and suddenly remembered her serene, sculptured face in the kitchen that first day, so poised and yet so warm and engaging. Even then, she had glimpsed her own fleeting reflection, and felt a kind of intuition that Rukhsana held the key to something inside Yasmin herself. As they hugged each other close, she was aware of the waiting silence downstairs. She knew it was not going to be easy facing the world outside Rukhsana's warm cherishing embrace, a world that began in the room below. But she realised she had felt a quiet strength flowing between them from those first fascinating encounters.

"We'll be fine together," Rukhsana encouraged softly, echoing her thoughts. "Come on, let's hit the world!" They exchanged a laughing, flurried kiss and turned to leave the room.

GLOSSARY

aloo gobi	- potato and cauliflower dish
ammi	- mummy/mum
bahji	- big sister
beti	- daughter
bhangra	- Asian disco dance music
biryani	- rice dish
burfi	- Indian milk sweet
chapattis	- flat, thin, unleavened bread
chup!	- shush!
dahi raita	- yoghurt with cucumber and spices
Diwali	- Hindu and Sikh festival
dhurrie	- cotton rug
dupatta	- long scarf of thin material
gori	- white woman
gulab jaman	- spongy sweet soaked in syrup
halal meat	- meat from animals slaughtered according to the prescriptions of the Koran
kohl	- black eye-lining powder
kurta	- long-sleeved tunic
Ramadan	- Muslim month of fasting
roti	- chapatti (cooked over an open flame)
shalwar kameez	- Punjabi-style trousers and long tunic
tabla	- pair of small drums played with the hands
tawa	- slightly concave griddle for making chapattis
topi	- an Indian hat